Just
Wanna
Testify

Just Wanna Testify

A NOVEL

Pearl Cleage

ONE WORLD

BALLANTINE BOOKS   NEW YORK

Published in the United States by One World Books, an imprint of The Random House Publishing Group, a division of Random House, Inc., New York.

ONE WORLD is a registered trademark and the One World colophon is a trademark of Random House, Inc.

Cleage, Pearl.
    Just wanna testify : a novel / Pearl Cleage.
        p. cm.
    ISBN 978-0-345-50636-8 (hardcover) — ISBN 978-0-345-52624-3 (ebook)
    1. African American women—Fiction. 2. Atlanta (Ga.)—Fiction. I. Title.
    PS3553.L389J87 2011
    813'.54—dc22   2010050945

Printed in the United States of America

www.oneworldbooks.net

9 8 7 6 5 4 3 2 1

First Edition

Book design by Diane Hobbing

For Zaron, who still makes me wanna testify

And for Bailey, Chloe, Michael, Deignan, and Will,
who make me want to live forever

There is a land of the living and a land of the dead and the bridge is love, the only survival, the only meaning.
　　　　—THORNTON WILDER, *The Bridge of San Luis Rey*

I just wanna testify
what your love has done for me.

　　　　　　　　　　　—PARLIAMENT

Prologue

When Regina Hamilton found out she was pregnant with her second child, she was so happy that she cried. She cried again when she called to tell her Aunt Abbie and one more time that night when she told Blue. By the time they told Sweetie that she was going to be a big sister, Regina's tears had stopped flowing, but she couldn't stop smiling. Blue teased her about it, but she could tell he was really happy, too. She accused him of liking her best when she was barefoot and pregnant, and he said he didn't know about the barefoot part, but loving her when she was carrying their child was about as close to heaven as he could stand to get.

That brought on a brief relapse in the crying department, but it didn't last. She smiled all the way through her first trimester and now seemed to be sleeping her way through the second. If she didn't get in an afternoon nap, she couldn't keep her eyes open after eight o'clock. This put her on the same four-year-old's sleep schedule as her daughter and also put a serious crimp in her late night love life. Blue just laughed and reminded her that she'd be back on a more adult schedule in another couple of weeks and then they could make up for lost time.

Regina couldn't wait that long. She arranged a sleepover for Sweetie, turned off the phone, and took a two-hour nap, then made reservations at Landon's and went out and bought a new dress that complemented her pregnancy curves. Blue's eyes when he saw her in it let her know that he didn't want to wait either. They lingered over the meal, enjoying a night out together, but when their server offered dessert, they both declined so quickly, Regina felt herself blush like a teenager.

Blue took her arm gently and guided her across the parking lot, which was rapidly filling up with cars of hungry people. The chef at Landon's knew his way around the kitchen and the place had a growing number of enthusiastic regulars.

"You could have had dessert if you wanted it," Regina said as Blue backed the big black Lincoln out carefully and turned the car onto Cascade Road. "I had a nap this afternoon. I'm good until midnight!"

That made him laugh and she did, too. In front of them, the moon rose, glowing at the end of the street like a giant yellow ball.

"My God," Regina said. "It looks close enough to touch."

"My mother used to call that a Cascade Moon."

"I've been here six years and I've never seen a moon like that."

"It's rare," Blue said. "Something to do with the rotation of the earth."

"Doesn't everything have to do with the rotation of the earth?"

"Exactly."

It looked like a movie moon. She half expected E.T. and that little kid on the bicycle to come pedaling across her view. Regina couldn't take her eyes off it.

"Is it good luck?"

He shrugged. "I don't remember her saying anything about it being lucky. Mostly it was supposed to be a time when spirits walk."

"What kind of spirits?"

"Only the restless ones," he said, reaching over to squeeze her knee lightly, but keeping his eyes on the road.

"Don't laugh," she said, covering his hand with her own so he would leave it where it was. "I was over at the Growers Association today and ShaRhonda and Lu were talking about vampires. Do they count?"

The Growers Association was the organization behind West End's impressive network of one hundred community gardens. Their headquarters was the nerve center of the neighborhood and Regina stopped by daily to catch up on the news.

Blue raised his eyebrows. "Vampires in West End?"

"No, but just about everywhere else, to hear them tell it. Lu was teasing ShaRhonda about having a crush on some movie vampire guy who can't have sex with his girlfriend because he might lose control and start sucking her blood."

Blue shook his head slowly. "Now, that is a brother with a serious problem."

"I can't imagine why they would think that was sexy."

"Probably because they've never had sex."

"Good sex anyway," Regina said.

"Bad sex doesn't count," Blue said, his smile half hidden in his mustache.

She smiled back. "You got that right."

As Cascade Road turned into Abernathy Boulevard, West End's main business artery, late shoppers could be seen hurrying home with whatever couldn't wait until tomorrow, as students strolled back to their dorms clutching take-out cups of cappuccino from the West End News. Nobody seemed to be paying much attention to the moon, which was still glowing like a lighthouse as they turned down Peeples Street and pulled up in front of their house. The huge magnolia that dominated their front yard looked ghostly against the night sky.

"I would hate that," Regina said, leaning her head against his shoulder as they started up the front walk, arm in arm.

"Hate what, baby?"

"Vampires in West End."

Blue laughed softly and opened the big front door. "That will never happen."

"How can you be so sure?" she said, stepping out of her heels.

"Because these vampires know I don't play that stuff."

"Good," she said, nuzzling his neck, trying unsuccessfully to stifle a great big yawn.

"You still good till midnight?"

"Absolutely!" she said, heading upstairs. "Don't keep me waiting!"

The water felt good against her skin as she took a quick shower, while Blue closed up the house for the night. Slipping under the sheets wearing nothing but her favorite perfume, she wondered what it would feel like to be in love with Blue and not be able to make love to him. She doubted that she could do it, no matter what the risks might be.

She shivered a little at the cool cotton sheets against her skin. *Good thing I don't believe in vampires.* She yawned sleepily and closed her eyes, listening for Blue's footsteps in the hallway, never knowing that by the time he slid in beside her, she was already snoring softly, one arm laid protectively across the gentle swell of her belly, smiling and dreaming. . . .

Just
Wanna
Testify

Chapter One

Miss Jada Don't Play That

Friday

At last! Serena thought, taking one last look in the mirror. *They have recognized how good I am at what I do!*

She was known for her patience, her ability to wait her turn, but the last thing she needed was one more boring modeling assignment. Finally, they had handed her something she could really sink her teeth into. It was about time. Six feet tall *before* stepping into her five-inch, stiletto-heel boots and startlingly slender, Serena had a strange, otherworldly beauty that she enhanced by pulling her long, dark hair away from her face, emphasizing her high, sharp cheekbones, her almond-shaped eyes, and the bright red slash of her mouth, always painted crimson.

Modeling had been a perfect cover for her and the others, who looked enough like Serena to be her sisters. They had been given unlimited access to any men they fancied, which was great, but lately they had become so well known that it was hard to move around without drawing a crowd of pain-in-the-ass innocent by-standers, which was never a good thing. She had been assured that once they successfully completed their Atlanta assignment, the modeling cover would be honorably retired from service.

Serena was glad to hear it and she had every intention of success-fully completing her mission. There was no room for distractions. When her superiors told her that she was going to Atlanta for a few weeks, they repeated the usual warnings about all things male, but there was no need to worry. Serena had waited too long for an as-signment like this. Romance was the last thing on her agenda.

It wasn't that Serena didn't believe in love. She just hadn't been raised to seek it, need it, or trust it. The stories that the women in her family passed along from one generation to the next all warned of the destructive power of making bad choices in matters of the heart. They stressed the dangers of opening her door, or her legs, to a man to whom their ideas of love and honor were no more than musings in a foreign-sounding tongue.

That's what she'd been taught by those much wiser than she was. And who was she to question them? It was that wisdom that had helped their little group survive when so many others like them had disappeared. Besides, she was not a politician or a philosopher or a social scientist. She was simply an agent with a nonnegotiable con-tract to enforce that had been willingly and freely signed by all par-ties, including those young fools from Morehouse who had been living like kings all over Atlanta for the last four years. Now it was time for them to hold up their end of the bargain. They had been in-structed to show up on campus this morning to finalize the details of their agreement. She and her team would be there, shooting an *Essence* magazine cover spread, but that's exactly what it was: a *cover.* Their real assignment had nothing to do with fashion and everything to do with survival.

Serena wondered if the boys would try to weasel out of it. She assumed that they would, but that was neither here nor there. They would be no match for the team she was bringing with her. Scylla was the best possible second-in-command and had trained the girls relentlessly until Serena was confident they could perform efficiently no matter what challenges they might have to face. One way or another, the five guys whose names were on her list had a trip to a very private island in their future.

Showtime, Serena thought, giving her hair one more pat and opening the door to the living room of the suite at the Four Seasons hotel that she would be sharing with Scylla for the next seven days. Already dressed head to toe in black, as was Serena, Scylla was standing in the center of the room, staring a the giant flat-screen TV.

"Time to go?" Scylla said, without taking her eyes off the screen where a dancing couple was swooping and gliding around the floor, baring their blindingly white teeth at each other and faking as much sexual energy as they could, under the circumstances.

"We've got a few minutes," Serena said, glancing at her watch and heading for the small wet bar in the corner where there were several bottles of Bloody Mary mix and a fifth of Absolut. "I'm going to drop you off and then stop by and pay my respects to Blue Hamilton. Have you had your cocktail?"

It was a rhetorical question, so she didn't wait for an answer, as she reached for two glasses and dropped in ice cubes from the polished silver bucket nearby. She opened the vodka and poured a splash in each glass. She was sick of tomato juice, but the vodka made it a little more tolerable. Her hands moved quickly and efficiently, as if she could perform these bartending chores in her sleep.

On the screen, an embarrassed actor, way past his sexual prime, was trying to catch his breath after executing a laughable attempt at a mambo.

"What are you watching?"

"*Dancing with the Stars.*"

"At seven thirty in the morning?"

Scylla waggled the remote in Serena's direction. "On demand," she said. "In case you missed it."

Serena stirred their drinks delicately with a plastic swizzle stick, carried both glasses across the room, and set one down in front of Scylla, who took a small sip.

"We should be on there," Scylla said, nodding at the screen.

"*Dancing with the Stars*?" Serena shook her head. "No thanks."

"Don't knock it. Maybe they would let us all compete together. Sort of in a group."

"No, probably not. Just you."

"You think they'd let me pick my own partner?"

"I don't see how they could stop you." Serena sat down and crossed her long legs and took a swallow of her drink. "Who did you have in mind? Brad Pitt?"

"Yeah, right," Scylla said sarcastically. "Like Angelina is going to let his pussy-whipped ass come out and dance with us."

"She gave us an island instead of her man," Serena said, as a liquid shrug rippled her slender shoulders like a breeze. "What are you gonna do?"

"How about Will Smith?" Scylla said, but Serena just raised an eyebrow.

"You know Miss Jada don't play that."

Scylla turned toward Serena with an expression that was almost hopeful. "She's not with us, is she?"

Serena shook her head and took another swallow of her Bloody Mary. "No way. What made you think that?"

"Well, you know she's got that punk band, Wicked Wisdom. Black leather. Scientology."

"She's not a Scientologist."

"Too bad," Scylla said, shaking her head a little. "That would make it easier to ask her if we can use her husband to jump-start things."

"It's the Mormons who are into polygamy."

"I know, but the Scientologists have that frozen sperm thing, right? What we're asking isn't any weirder than that."

Serena looked at her friend. "This feels so familiar, doesn't it? Like old times?"

"Don't get sentimental on me," Scylla said, reaching over.to pat Serena's hand briskly like a mother telling a toddler to buck up on the first day of nursery school. "We've got a job to do, remember?"

Serena saw no reason to respond to that. She was in charge of this mission. Forgetting about the job was not an option. They watched a not very interesting quickstep from a lackluster couple who seemed tired of the show and of each other.

"Do you think it's our fault?" Scylla said, taking another swallow of her drink. "About the men."

"What do you mean?"

"You know, all of them dying out like that at one time."

The judges were suggesting that the couple needed more practice. They agreed and promised to come back stronger next week, but everybody knew their steps were already numbered.

"I think it was the vibrators," Serena said, draining her glass and standing up. It was time to go.

Scylla frowned slightly, drained her glass, too, and clicked off the television. "What about the vibrators?"

"Once we got them perfected, it was a lot harder to get the girls to spend any time and energy on a real, live man. They just weren't as reliable." Serena went over to the closet and reached for her black trench coat. "Remember when they started issuing them as soon as we hit puberty?"

"Do I?" Scylla grabbed her big black shoulder bag and zipped up her black leather jacket. "On my thirteenth birthday, my mom gave me a box of Tampax and a pink vibrator as big as a baby's arm." She made a low, hissing sound like a snake sunning on a rock, and shook her head, remembering.

"What'd you do with it?"

"I followed the instructions on the back of the box," Scylla said, reaching for the door. "And the rest is *her*story."

"See, that's exactly what I'm talking about." Serena followed her out into the hallway.

The maid, slowly pushing her housekeeping cart down the long, empty hallway, seemed startled by the tall, alarmingly thin women striding in her direction, and she dropped her eyes and let them pass.

"We can pleasure ourselves, feed ourselves, lead ourselves," Serena said, punching the elevator Down button with a jab of her red-tipped finger. "All they had left to do was impregnate us and keep out of the way."

"Is that such a bad life?" Scylla said.

Serena turned back to her friend and arched her perfectly shaped eyebrows. "Would it be enough for you?"

"Of course not," Scylla said calmly. "But we're *women*. Men are different, remember?"

Chapter Two

Mingling with Humans

If there was one thing Blue Hamilton hated, it was a goddamn vampire, but there was no mistaking this one. He pulled into his usual space in front of the West End News and watched her. The girl was very tall and very thin and even sort of sexy in that weird, high-fashion kind of way. She was wearing tight black leather pants that hugged her almost boyish hips, a cropped, black leather bomber jacket, and a black turtleneck sweater. Her black suede boots ended at her thighs and seemed to be molded in such a way that they had no proper heel at all, requiring her to balance delicately on the balls of her feet, leaning slightly forward as she made her way down Ralph David Abernathy Boulevard like she belonged there. Which she most certainly did not.

When she stopped for the light at the corner across from the MARTA train station and tossed back her long dark hair, the incense and T-shirt vendors, who were never at a loss for words, just stood unblinking until she was too far away to hear them, not a single one able to gather his wits about him and offer the usual spiel. Somehow, they seemed to know she was out of their league and they let her glide by without so much as a, "Good mornin', sistah! You're lookin' lovely today, mah queen!"

Blue sighed as she turned out of sight. Everywhere he looked these days, he was confronted with glamorous images of ghostly vamps mingling with humans in New York and certain neighborhoods in L.A., like there was nothing strange about it at all. Vamps is what he called them and vamps is what they were. Lean, mean, sexy girls, pale as the belly of a bigmouth bass. Slim hipped and staring with what would have been soulful eyes, except these lithe creatures had no souls. That was the whole point. They were the undead and now they were roaming around Atlanta like it was suddenly a suburb of Beverly Hills.

It was only a matter of time before one of them strolled into the West End News, looking for a cappuccino. The problem was, nobody suspected that their sudden ubiquity was anything more than the latest craze of a death-obsessed culture. Nobody thought they were real. Nobody except Blue. He knew that these girls—and the real ones were all girls—were here for a reason. But what was it?

Sometimes Blue missed the old days when the gangstas and the crackheads were as deep as it got. He had known how to deal with them, and West End had become an oasis of peace and civility even as things continued to spiral out of control all over the country and all over the world. The West End News carried papers from everywhere, but Blue hardly spent the time it took to read the front pages anymore. The stories were all the same. War, disease, famine, rape, genocide, and territorial disputes over water and oil and drugs and whatever else somebody thought they needed bad enough to take somebody's life for it.

Blue was different. The people he had eliminated from West End over the years had been guilty of such heinous crimes that no one could argue that justice had not been served. Prostituting children.

Torturing women. Raping mothers in front of their sons. When the guys responsible for those crimes disappeared from the scene, nobody was sorry. Even their mothers were relieved as they closed their eyes and clasped their hands and said a little prayer for the souls of their babies gone bad. But these vampires were a whole other thing. Slinking around in their tight black clothes and their bright red lips, they had no one to pray for them, which probably suited them just fine. How do you pray for something that has no soul?

Blue stepped out of the car and looked around at his neighborhood on its way to work. Everybody worked in West End. If you couldn't find a job, Blue found one for you. Of course if you wanted to spend your time hustling dope, pimping women, or watching porno in your grandmomma's basement, you had every right to do that. You just couldn't do it in West End.

"Hey, Mr. Blue!" a woman called as she headed over to the twenty-four-hour beauty salon. "Why you gotta be so sharp this early in the morning?"

Blue smiled and touched his fingertips lightly to the front of his perfectly blocked Homburg. He was aware that it gave him an immediate visual advantage to appear on the streets of West End dressed in the manner made famous by Michael Corleone in *The Godfather*: black silk suit, blindingly white shirt, black cashmere coat, black hat, and highly polished shoes. It was a uniform that conferred the authority of a mythical movie gangster who was a role model even to small-time thugs whose crimes were no more organized than anything else they did.

The place was already full when Blue walked in. The West End News was a popular coffee shop and well-stocked newsstand, and Blue's base of operations, maintained from a suite of rooms in the back where no one ventured without an invitation and an escort. Behind the counter, Henry Graham, his right-hand man, and Phoebe Sanderson, who'd been working there part-time since high school, were making cups of perfect cappuccino and teasing the regulars who stopped in for their daily fix of caffeine and gossip. When he looked up and saw Blue, Henry nodded imperceptibly and Phoebe followed his eyes to the door.

"Good morning, Mr. Hamilton," she said cheerfully, as Henry took off his big white apron and reached for his suit jacket hanging nearby. He wore lots of hats at the West End News. With his shaved head and unlined face, it was hard to gauge his actual age, but he seemed to be a pleasant, muscular man of about forty. When he was behind the counter, he always wore a white apron over a crisp white shirt and dark tie. When Blue arrived, all he had to do was take off the apron, slip on his coat, and be suddenly transformed into a successful businessman or a particularly well-dressed bodyguard, depending on which part of Henry's story you heard from somebody who acted like he knew.

"Good morning to you, Ms. Sanderson," Blue said, removing his hat with a small formal nod in her direction and a general smile for the starstruck patrons who knew that a sho' nuff Blue Hamilton sighting was the best watercooler story anybody would have that day, no matter who had won the celebrity dance-off the night before. It wasn't that he didn't make himself visible around the West End News frequently. It was simply that the way he moved through with such mysterious cool, once he was gone, folks could never be sure they'd seen him at all.

"How's business this morning?"

Phoebe grinned. "Couldn't be better."

"Good." Blue nodded approvingly while Henry moved to stand at his side. "Don't know what we're going to do without you when you head back up to school."

"Maybe I won't go back," she said, teasing him because she could. "Maybe I'll open another coffee shop down the street and give you and Henry some competition."

"I'll look forward to it," Blue said, moving toward the rear of the store. "Morning, everybody."

"Good morning, Mr. Hamilton," his customers said in unison like a well-trained group of fifth graders greeting their homeroom teacher, their eyes following him and Henry until they disappeared down the short hallway. Outside the smoked-glass doorway to the private suite, Henry paused and laid a hand on Blue's arm.

"What's wrong?" Blue's voice was a low, melodic rumble that had earned him a place in R & B history as a young hit maker when he was only seventeen and later as a fabled live performer who had such an electrifying effect on women that they had been known to faint at his feet.

"There's already someone waiting to see you, Mr. Hamilton. I thought it was better to let her wait back here."

Blue frowned and slipped out of his overcoat, handing it to Henry along with the Homburg. He wasn't expecting visitors this morning, and certainly no strange females. "Alone?"

"Jake's with her."

"What does she want?"

"I don't know," Henry said, shrugging his massive shoulders. "But she looks . . . different."

"Different how?"

Henry didn't blink. "Just different."

"Okay," Blue said. "Well, let's see what's on her mind."

The woman's back was to the door when Blue opened it and stepped inside, nodding at Jake who immediately withdrew from his post and joined Henry in the hallway outside, pulling the door closed silently behind him. The woman, wearing a long black trench coat and black stilettos, didn't move. Tall and alarmingly slender, she was standing in front of a large-framed black-and-white photograph of two little girls who had grown up around the corner. She appeared unaware that anyone had entered the room.

"They will be freshmen at Spelman in the fall," he said.

At the sound of his voice, she turned around slowly and Blue found himself face-to-face with the finest vamp he had ever seen. Her large dark eyes were heavily lined in black, and her hair was pulled back into a tight knot. Her golden skin was nothing like the usual pallor of her kind, but with that slash of red mouth and that emaciated frame, there was no mistaking what she was.

"I'm Blue Hamilton."

"I'm Serena Mayflower," she said without a smile. "I've been waiting for you."

Chapter Three

Cutting Edge

Regina didn't call her friend before she walked the four blocks from her house to Aretha's studio on the top floor of the four-unit building where Blue still kept an apartment across the hall. Downstairs, Abbie conducted her visionary workshops on one side, and on the other, Blue maintained a fully furnished guest suite that he made available to a small circle of trusted friends, usually musicians looking for a place to rest up from the road and maybe jam a little if Blue was in the mood.

At the moment, it was empty. Blue was at the West End News and Abbie was getting ready to head to Tybee Island for a few days, so Regina knew the sound of Bob Marley could be coming only from Aretha's place.

"There's a natural mystic, blowing through the air . . ."

Regina smiled to herself. This was such a familiar scene it was almost déjà vu. The day she'd arrived in West End, looking for an apartment, she had wandered around enjoying the carefully tended yards and blossoming pink dogwood trees. Watching women walking with their children past men who nodded their heads or tipped their hats and said good morning, she felt almost as if she had fallen down the rabbit hole and emerged in some kind of Afro-urban paradise. No wonder she didn't remember seeing any For Rent signs. Who wouldn't want to live in a neighborhood like this one?

Turning down Lawton Street that day, she had heard Marley's voice then, too, and followed the sound like a moth to a shimmering, dreadlocked flame. When she located the source and stopped out front to listen, she remembered thinking how perfect this building with the bright blue front door would be if only it had a vacancy. That's when Blue Hamilton opened that very same door, and said that he owned the building and she could move in immediately if she wanted to, which, of course, she did.

That was also the day she met Aretha Hargrove. When Regina first arrived in West End, Aretha was a young artist just finding her vision, always engaged in projects about which she remained passionate even as she moved on to the next one. The Door Project was one of the most visible and it was in full swing the day the two women met. Aretha had recently read a book that said some North African people believed painting the front door a certain shade of turquoise was the best way to ward off the evil eye. The same article also said that getting small children to make handprints in the wet paint increased the effectiveness of the mojo.

Aretha went to Blue and proposed painting the front doors of all his properties as part of a project that would be both aesthetically pleasing and possibly spiritually significant. Blue agreed, although he drew the line at the handprints, and Aretha did about fifteen or twenty doors before a rumor started that those blue front doors signified a special relationship with Mr. Hamilton, which set in motion so many requests for the doors that Aretha had to hire a crew just to keep up.

The project even drew a television news crew to the area, curious about this quiet, well-maintained little neighborhood, just a few minutes away from downtown Atlanta and unknown to almost everybody who didn't live there. That was, of course, the way Blue liked it. When a second news crew showed up, he suggested that perhaps Aretha could find a less public way to keep any demons at bay and she agreed. But the blue doors were still a unique feature of West End, like the hex signs on the barns in Pennsylvania Dutch country, and Aretha still got requests regularly from people who wanted one, or who had one that needed a little touching up around the edges.

This one sure didn't need any touching up, Regina thought, heading up the front walk. It was practically glowing with a fresh coat of paint that was almost exactly the color of her husband's eyes. The outside door wasn't locked. She knew it wouldn't be. Nobody ever had to lock a door in West End. The neighborhood hadn't had a rape, robbery, or homicide in more than a decade.

That was one of the things Regina loved and admired about Blue, even though she still worried sometimes about the role he had taken on. He hadn't just complained about the sorry state of too many African American communities, he had fixed one. He had stepped up, moved in, and taken control. He had demanded a high level of personal responsibility from the men and women who lived there, and in return he had promised that he would provide the necessary protection they needed to reclaim their community. And he did.

At the top of the stairs, Aretha's door was open into the hallway. Bob Marley had moved from the purely mystical to the sweetly sensual, but Aretha herself was standing at her worktable laying out the equipment she would need for the first day's shoot, which included five cameras: two digital; one old, large format for portraits; another old Polaroid for test shots; and her beloved Leica, which always hung around her neck more like a talisman than a tool of her trade. Aretha liked to work here even though she and her daughter, Joyce

Ann, lived in a little house a few blocks away that had plenty of room for a studio. She loved the light, she told Blue when she asked him if it was okay to take over the space when Regina moved out.

What she didn't say, because somehow she felt he already knew, was that she needed a space where she wasn't required to be anything other than an artist. A free space where she could go wherever her imagination nudged her without having to stop for spelling homework or dinner dishes or the mailman at the door.

Aretha was so focused on the task at hand that she didn't even notice Regina smiling in the open door.

"You know where I can find a hotshot fashion photographer around here?"

Aretha looked over her shoulder and threw up her hands. "This is a terrible idea! I don't know why I let you talk me into this," she wailed.

"I never talked you into anything and you know it," Regina said soothingly.

"But you didn't talk me out of it."

Aretha never played up her looks, but even when she was agitated, Aretha's beauty was undeniable. She wore her hair cropped very close, which drew attention to her big, dark eyes with their long, thick lashes. Tall and athletically built, she had a strong nose and full lips that turned up at the corners just enough to make people think she had a secret worth telling. Aretha looked like a model herself, Regina thought, if models looked like the very best that real people had to offer instead of another species all together.

"You're mad at me for not talking you out of doing an *Essence* cover spread with the hottest models on the planet?"

"Listen to yourself," Aretha groaned. "How can you even say the words *hottest models on the planet* and not gag?"

"Because, my high-strung friend, my finder's fee for setting up this little gig is enough to buy three computers for Sweetie's kindergarten class."

Aretha looked at Regina, who smiled angelically.

"That's right, throw the kids up at me."

"I only threw my own." Regina laughed. "But if I need to add Princess Joyce Ann to the mix, I will."

Joyce Ann was a huge fan of the Disney princesses line and anytime she had a say in the matter, she would don one costume or another, from tiara to slippers, and move among her family and friends with what can only be described as a decidedly regal demeanor. Accordingly, Aretha's friends had begun to call her daughter *Princess,* over her laughing objections that if they weren't prepared to move in and function as her highness's ladies-in-waiting, they needed to stay out of it. Blue and Regina's daughter, Sweetie (whose real name was Juanita, but who had been Sweetie since the first time her daddy held her in his arms and pronounced her "the sweetest baby girl ever") idolized Joyce Ann and had already inherited a few precious gowns after the original princess outgrew them.

"All right," Aretha said, "you win. But you better stay close enough to keep reminding me this is all for a good cause." She picked up the old portrait camera and fit it carefully into a silver camera case lined in gray foam with cutout spaces for its precious cargo.

"That's what I'm here for," Regina said. "You don't think I'd let you have this adventure without me in my own backyard, do you? I told Blue this morning not to expect to see me around much until you were done shooting."

Aretha was stalking around the small space, grabbing all manner of expensive-looking equipment that Regina couldn't begin to identify by form or function and tucking it firmly into her various camera cases. There was clearly a method to her madness, but Regina couldn't have said what it was. She decided her best course of action was to stay out of the way.

"I thought you were up for this. What happened?"

"*What happened?* I met them, that's what happened!" She stopped moving around and shook her head. "You should see these girls, Gina. They are positively creepy!"

Regina perched herself on the edge of a tall stool. She knew Aretha didn't approve of the whole cult of skinny that dominated high fashion around the world, but she also knew Aretha was nervous. This was a big assignment and Aretha was not technically a fashion photographer. A friend of Regina's who worked at *Essence* had been setting up an Atlanta photo shoot and they wanted to use Aretha. They were going to shoot it on and around the Morehouse College campus to play up the contrast between serious young scholars and the more extreme fall fashions. The models' agent had specifically requested her. Since Aretha didn't have a New York agent, Regina was happy to facilitate, knowing that if this went well, Aretha would have more offers than she knew what to do with. It had been a moment when Regina's business head had been as important as Aretha's artistic eye.

"They're an international phenomenon," Regina said. "Did you look at the magazines I put in your mailbox yesterday?"

"Did *you*?" Aretha said indignantly, her long silver earrings swaying against the graceful arch of her neck.

"They're cutting edge."

Aretha snorted derisively as she tucked one more camera snugly into its foam cocoon and closed the silver suitcase carefully. "Cutting edge, my foot. They look like a bunch of heroin addicts. Vampires! That's what they look like. A bunch of vampires. They're all about eight feet tall and they weigh about fifty pounds, max. I met them for dinner last night and you know what they ate? Nothing! Nada! Zip! Zilch! Tomato juice! They all drank tomato juice!"

"They're models. What do you expect?"

"I'm serious, Gina. These girls are entirely too thin. What kind of body image is that putting forward to Joyce Ann and Sweetie?"

"Last time I checked," Regina said calmly, "Joyce Ann and Sweetie weren't reading *Essence*."

"Not yet," Aretha said ominously, adding another camera case to the other equipment waiting by the door.

"Where are they staying?"

"Who knows? They won't need room service, that's for sure."

Aretha was standing in the center of the room with her hands on her hips, looking around to be sure she didn't miss anything she might need once the shoot got started. Morehouse was only ten minutes away, but she didn't want to have to come back for anything. Seemingly satisfied that everything was ready to go, she turned back to Regina, still agitated.

"This is all Angelina Jolie's fault, you know that? Slinking around in all that black leather, wearing her husband's blood in a vial around her neck. That was exactly where it all started, trust me."

"Her *first* husband's blood."

"Actually, Billy Bob was her *second* husband, but all I'm saying is, if I was Brad Pitt, I'd watch my back."

"Or your neck."

"Go to hell!" Aretha said, lobbing an empty film canister at Regina, who laughed and ducked out of the way. She had been around Aretha at work enough to know that her friend tended to work herself into a kind of creative frenzy and then hurl herself at the project in question like a ball of uncontained, artistic energy. That was just her process, Blue said, and so far, it had been working like a charm. All Regina had to do was hang on for the ride.

"You ready?"

Aretha sighed and rolled her eyes. "Say your line."

"It's for a good cause."

"Say it again."

"It's for a good cause, and if you give it half a chance, it might even be fun, in addition to opening up all kinds of new professional opportunities for you."

"Now you sound like my agent for real."

"Real agents don't help you schlep your stuff," Regina said, reaching for the smallest of the silver cases.

"Then what do they do?" Aretha said, grabbing the rest of the equipment and heading downstairs to her bright red pickup parked out front.

They settled the equipment first and then climbed in and buckled up.

"They take care of business so you can concentrate on being an artist," Regina said, closing the door behind them. "And they remind you that you're a genius, in case you ever forget it."

"Not a chance," Aretha said, grinning over at Regina for the first time that morning.

"Good," Regina said. "Then let's go take some pictures!"

Chapter Four

Available Men

Serena Mayflower declined Blue Hamilton's offer of a cup of espresso and cleared her throat delicately, as she took the seat he offered her.

"Thank you so much for agreeing to see me, Mr. Hamilton," she said softly. "I know you're a very busy man."

Blue decided there was no reason to point out that he hadn't really agreed or disagreed, since she had arrived unannounced seeking an audience. He said nothing.

"But since we're going to be doing business in West End for a couple of days, I thought I owed you a courtesy call."

"What business are you in?"

"I manage a group of five high-fashion models. You may have seen them on some of the magazine covers out front? They're hot all over the world right now."

"I see," Blue said. "What brings you to West End?"

"We're working with a brilliant young photographer who happens to be one of your neighbors. Aretha Hargrove?"

He inclined his head slightly in the direction of the photo she'd been studying so intently when he walked in. "That's one of her pictures hanging right behind you."

"I thought so," Serena said, without turning away from Blue. "There's something so *alive* about her work."

Strange choice of words for the undead, Blue thought.

"Did Aretha tell you to come see me?"

Serena hesitated. "Well, actually she did. She told us all about you at dinner last night."

Blue doubted that. "I see."

The silence between them lengthened and Serena had the feeling he could sit there as long as she could without speaking. Maybe longer. The ball was definitely in her court. She cleared her throat again.

"We'll be shooting primarily on the Morehouse campus," she said, "which I understand from Aretha is *technically* not a part of your . . . *territory*. But I hope we'll be able to do some shots around here, too. I'm absolutely in love with all the blue doors."

"They're intended to ward off evil spirits," Blue said.

Serena looked at him, and if she had been capable of smiling, she probably would have. "Do they work?"

"You tell me." Blue's voice was suddenly a low warning rumble.

She raised her dark, pencil thin, perfectly arched eyebrows. "Excuse me?"

"I know what you are."

"Don't you mean *who*?" she said, crossing her long slender legs, and letting her coat fall open to be sure Blue saw the flash of thigh her short, black leather skirt revealed. Blue's eyes never left her face.

"Ms. Mayflower, if Aretha told you where to find me, she must have also told you I'm not a man who enjoys playing games."

Serena reached for her coat and pulled it back over her legs quickly, glancing away for the first time. "I'm sorry, Mr. Hamilton.

It's just . . . you just . . . your eyes just make me a little nervous. I don't quite know where to begin."

Blue's expression didn't change. Here he was standing toe-to-toe with a damn vampire and *he* made *her* nervous. So far, so good.

"Is there somewhere we can talk?"

"Aren't we already talking?" Blue said.

"Yes, I suppose we are."

She folded her long, thin hands on the table. Each perfectly tapered nail was polished the same bright red as her lipstick.

"Let me first address any safety concerns you might have," she said in her breathy whisper. "Yes, we are who we are, but the danger we used to present to . . . people was eliminated many years ago when we discovered an easily available substitute substance that does away completely with our desire for . . . certain kinds of protein."

"What's the substance?"

"Tomato juice."

He almost laughed out loud. "Tomato juice?"

She looked a little embarrassed as she nodded. "It's almost a cliché, I suppose, but it works. And as you know, tomato products are easy to get everywhere. We used to grow our own back in New Orleans—that's where we're from, right outside New Orleans. We lived in peace with the locals there for many generations, but after the hurricane, conditions just became intolerable, so we had to move. Fortunately, a friend of ours provided us with a lovely little private island where we can rebuild our lives unmolested."

Serena was choosing her words carefully as if he were going to cross-examine her later, although in a sense, he already was.

"Go on."

"The only problem is, it's a tiny little island with no business or industry, so we have to come over to the mainland periodically to make money and pick up the things we need." She shrugged with a strange rippling motion of her slender shoulders. "Then we go back."

"Some of you don't go back," Blue said, wondering if she would admit it.

She fluttered her thick black lashes, and he thought that maybe she had deluded herself into thinking she had more information than he did. "Some of us find lives or partners here that we prefer to our more monastic life on the island."

"Why monastic?"

"Our society is strongly matrilineal, Mr. Hamilton. Men have always been rather peripheral to our lives. No offense," she added quickly.

"None taken."

"The men who used to partner with us in New Orleans were wiped out or displaced by the deluge and we haven't found any suitable substitutes."

Blue didn't know whether to offer sympathy or point her in the direction of some men who might be interested.

"The truth is, we've almost given up our search."

"And why is that?"

She leaned forward slightly. Her skin was so smooth it was almost translucent.

"Because," she said, looking at him without blinking, "we can't find any men with genes worthy of mixing with our own. No *available* men, anyway." And she fluttered her eyelashes again.

"I see."

"We both know, Mr. Hamilton, that there is always a moment when a species must adapt or die. Well, this is that crucial moment for our little tribe. We know it and, I assure you, we don't take it lightly."

He nodded slowly, wondering if they were incapable of smiling or if they just didn't choose to make the effort. "Does anyone else know of your presence here?"

Serena shook her dark, sleek head. "No."

"Good," he said, "I think that's best."

He knew he didn't have to tell her that mentioning even the possibility of vampires was liable to set off a wave of hysteria that was bad for the vamps and bad for West End. For several years he had managed to deflect inquiries and squash rumors about past lives and reincarnations, and until now the questions rarely arose. There was no need to stir up any renewed interest in the supernatural as it related to the mysterious Mr. Hamilton. In the public mind, people with past lives and people with endless lives were pretty much six of one, half dozen of the other. Keeping the vamp presence quiet was in both of their best interests.

"How long do you expect to be working in the neighborhood?"

"Another week at the most," she said. "Then we'll be on our way. We've got a shoot in Paris in ten days."

"That will be fine," Blue said, standing up so that she did, too. "Of course, I will provide security for you and your team while you're here with us."

"Thank you," she said. "That will be greatly appreciated. I'll be sure to get you a list of our locations."

"That won't be necessary," Blue said. "I already have it."

She looked at him for a beat without blinking, then picked up her big black bag and slung it over her shoulder. "Then I guess our business is done."

He wondered briefly how she could get around in those high heels. A cracked sidewalk or an errant tree root would cripple this girl for life. He walked her to the door and reached for the knob. On the other side of the smoked glass, he could see Henry and Jake waiting just outside.

"I appreciate you taking the time to stop by and introduce yourself," he said. "And I hope you will call on me if you need any further assistance while you're here."

"Thank you," she said, and held out her hand. It was smooth when he shook it and colder than he thought it would be.

"Good morning, Mr. Hamilton," she said softly, pulling on a pair of black kid gloves. She was tall enough to look him in the eyes and she did.

"Good morning, Ms. Mayflower."

Henry was waiting to walk her back through the café. Jake nodded and held his post right outside the door where he would remain throughout the day.

Blue closed the door behind her slowly and sat back down. Grown women had been coming on to him since he was fourteen. They had thrown their panties at him on the stage, slipped him their phone numbers and hotel room keys, stolen his sweat-drenched costumes after shows, and regularly asked him for his autograph on the street even now, but this was the very first time he'd ever been flirted with by a vampire. He had a feeling that it wouldn't be the last. He reached into his breast pocket for the phone and punched in Abbie's number.

Chapter Five

In Search of Models

The models weren't due on set until ten o'clock, but when Aretha pulled her truck up to the front entrance of King Chapel at quarter to nine, there was already a small but growing crowd of Morehouse students gathering across the street in front of the Student Center. They were trying to look casual, but it was pretty obvious that they had come to see the Too Fine Five, celebrity shorthand for the models that Aretha was there to photograph.

Dressed in everything from their best Sunday suits to their favorite oversized jeans and big white T-shirts, they were all pretending that they were there just to see what was going on, not hoping to be picked to be a part of it. The models' appeal to the young men in the African American urban community was in some ways an anomaly, considering that there was nothing on any of the women's bodies remotely resembling a booty, but several high-profile rappers had put them in videos that featured big yachts, expensive cars, exclusive resort hotels, and pristine private beaches. Their job was to stand or lounge around looking bored and vaguely spectral while the sexual energy of the headliner raged around them in all-too-human form.

They didn't really dance or even walk around very much. What they did was move to the music in a strangely arrhythmic motion that was oddly mesmerizing. Sometimes they'd slither around independently of one another, but then they'd all do the exact same gesture or movement at the exact same time, at no apparent signal, and freeze there for just a fraction of a second and then start moving again.

Across the country, boys watching the video were drawn to it in a way that made them laugh and tease one another about being under the power of those "weird skinny bitches," but they couldn't stop watching. Young men who had never seen these girls in a fashion photograph fantasized about having sex with them even as they realized that they probably would never have the nerve to approach one, much less all five, since one was rarely seen without the others.

"Pretty girls on an all-male campus." The public relations director had chuckled when Regina called to let him know that Blue would be sending over some people to round out the small campus police force. "The more security the better."

Aretha waved her thanks to the smiling campus police officer who removed the bright orange cones and let her pull right up beside the entrance to the chapel auditorium.

"Thanks, Sergeant," Aretha said, jumping out of the truck.

"Morning, Miss Hargrove," the smiling sergeant replied. "We got everything closed to traffic, just like you wanted. How you doin', Miz Hamilton?"

"I'm good," Regina said, slamming the door behind her and waiting for instructions from Aretha.

"I'm glad the weather cooperated," the sergeant said, nodding his approval of the cloudless Atlanta sky. The previous day had been chilly for late May and very wet. "It wouldn't do to have rain fallin' on these girls." He lowered his voice conspiratorially and winked. "They'd probably just wash right on away."

Aretha laughed, handing Regina the smallest camera case, which the sergeant immediately took from her. "I see their fans have already begun to gather in anticipation of their arrival."

"Anticipation, nothin'," he said, reaching up to get the larger case. "They have arrived."

"They're here already?"

He nodded. "Been here about an hour. Went straight downstairs."

Aretha looked annoyed. "How many of them were there?"

"Six all together," he said. "But only one of 'em talked."

"That would be the whole gaggle," she said as if they were a flock of migrating birds. "They're an hour early!"

"Probably on Milan time," Regina said quickly. "That means they are true professionals."

"So what does that make me?" Aretha snapped.

"An artist," Regina said, reaching for another case.

"Hang on, Miz Hargrove," the sergeant said, motioning to another officer standing nearby. "Let me get somebody to help you with that stuff."

"Thank you, Sergeant," she said, turning to Regina. "Do me a favor, will you? Go down there and make sure they've got everything they need, and I'll get things going up here."

"I'm on it," Regina said, heading for the big glass doors of the chapel in search of models.

She took the wide staircase down to the lower level, listening to see if they sounded like birds, too, since Aretha had described them that way, but they didn't. In fact, they didn't seem to be making any noise at all. Countless movie scenes of fashion shoots, from *Blow-Up* to *Sex and the City*, had conditioned Regina to expect to hear loud music as the fashion fantasy took shape under the hypercritical eyes of people who knew the difference between Prada and Dior.

But when she got to the bottom of the stairs, the first thing Regina noticed was how quiet it was. No music. No laughter. If she listened closely, she thought she could hear the sound of female voices murmuring somewhere nearby, but they were so quiet, she wasn't even sure where they were coming from. She headed in what she hoped was the right direction.

She had thought they were going to be using the small dressing rooms provided for speakers and performers, but the tiny cubicles had obviously not appealed to these women. Instead, someone had erected a kind of indoor tent for them in the large lobby space downstairs. It was constructed of diaphanous white fabric that fluttered softly in the artificial breeze coming from the building's ventilation system. Through the gently billowing fabric, Regina could see five ghostly, back-lit figures moving around slowly. They appeared to be very tall and very thin, except for two who were shorter and quicker and appeared to be helping the others into and out of their clothes.

"Looking for someone?"

The voice came from so close beside Regina's left shoulder, it made her jump. "You startled me!"

The woman standing in front of her didn't blink or apologize. "Security is supposed to be keeping people out of this area."

Regina was struck by how tall and thin this woman was, too. Her dark hair was pulled back so severely that it gave her face a stark, dramatic strangeness, and her neck was so long, it was as if her head was floating independent of her body. Regina had seen pictures of the models, but their manager—this had to be her in the flesh, what little there was of it—had been only a disembodied voice on the phone.

"I'm Regina Hamilton."

"Then you're looking for me," the woman said, extending a black-gloved hand. "Serena Mayflower."

"Welcome to Atlanta," Regina said, wondering if black leather gloves in May was the result of a cold nature or the latest fashion trend. "Aretha's upstairs getting things set up. She wanted me to make sure you have everything you need."

"We're fine," Serena said. "The *Essence* stylists are with them now making some final wardrobe decisions."

Regina assumed those would be the shorter, faster silhouettes behind the veil. "Did you bring hair and makeup people from New York, too?"

"They always do their own makeup," Serena said. "Our skin is very sensitive so we try not to be careless."

"That's pretty unusual, isn't it?" Regina said, surprised.

"It's unheard of," Serena said, "but we know what works for us and we stick with it."

The way she said *we* made Regina wonder if these women were related, but before she could ask, the white drapes were pushed aside and one of the models came out, looked around quickly, and then walked over to where they were standing. Regina had seen models before, but none as tall and skinny as this one. Everything on her was elongated, from her giraffelike neck to her mile-long legs. The closer she got, the taller she loomed, which made Regina think that she was going to have to tip back her head to say hello—like a little child being prompted to greet the pastor after church. She needn't have worried. Pleasantries were the last thing on this woman's mind.

"Look at this shit!" the model said, ignoring Regina completely and pointing one long, bony finger at her own head. "Scylla cannot be serious!"

She was wearing a pair of high-wasted pants, a tailored white shirt, and a pair of leopard-skin ankle boots with five-inch heels. Around her neck there were easily fifteen colorful beaded necklaces of various lengths. But the beautiful clothes and fanciful jewelry were not what you noticed first. It was her hair, which was dark, fuzzy, and abundant. For reasons that Regina figured were unfathomable to anyone outside the fashion world, someone had teased it out around her face in a wooly mushroom cloud that added another four or five inches to her already overwhelming height, creating an effect as startling as a brightly colored parrot coming to rest on the branches of a magnolia tree.

Serena looked at the agitated model without any discernable change of expression. "Scylla is always serious. You know that."

"Then she has lost her mind!"

"It's fine," Serena said calmly. "When you see the photos, you'll love it."

The model fluttered her hands unhappily around her hair without touching it and pouted her brightly painted red lips. "I will not love it. We look ridiculous."

"You look fabulous," Serena said. "Now stop fussing long enough to meet Regina Hamilton. Regina, this is Sasha, the baby of our group. We indulge her more than we should."

"Tell her," Sasha said, turning toward Regina and striking a Vogue-worthy pose. "Does this look like shit or not?"

It looked like nothing Regina had ever seen on a woman's head before, but Sasha didn't look like any woman she'd ever seen either, so the standards that normally applied were obviously useless.

"You look amazing," Regina said, and that was true.

Sasha snorted like that much was obvious. "We always look *amazing*. I'm talking about looking ridiculous."

A voice from the diaphanous tent joined the conversation. "Stop bitching and I'll let you do the makeup."

Sasha's pout disappeared and Regina had the feeling her expression was as close to a smile as the woman was going to get.

"For real?"

"Absolutely."

Serena paid no attention to the new voice at all. She looked bored.

"For the whole shoot?"

The curtains parted again to reveal another model. They looked enough alike in every way to be the twin daughters of some very odd-looking parents. She was wearing a gray pencil skirt and a hot-pink silk blouse with the same stacked necklaces and the same towering poof of hair. Regina wondered in what alternate universe this could be a college professor's classroom attire.

"For the rest of my fucking life, if you will just calm down and get back in here so we can get ready and go to work."

Sasha looked at Serena. "You're my witness. You heard that, right?"

"I heard it."

Seemingly satisfied with that less-than-enthusiastic response, Sasha sashayed back over to the billowing tent and brushed past the other model, who had now fixed her gaze on Regina.

"Scylla, meet Regina Hamilton. Regina, meet our creative director and resident genius. We couldn't do it without her."

"Nice to meet you," Regina said, trying not to stare. Standing among these women, she felt like a Georgia pine tree in the Sequoia National Forest trying to hold its own with the redwoods.

"Are you the agent?"

"Sort of," Regina said, smiling.

Scylla frowned. "What the hell does that mean? Are you the one we ought to talk to about doing the new portfolio or not?"

Before Regina could respond, Sasha raised her voice from behind the curtains, where she seemed to be standing over a woman perched on a high stool.

"Susan won't let me put the green eyeliner on her!"

"It looks stupid!" another voice cried from the inner sanctum.

Scylla sighed and glanced at Serena, then back to Regina like they had important unfinished business but she had no more time. "Does anybody around here know what the fuck they're doing?" she said, and ducked back behind the billowing fabric without another word.

Chapter Six

One Step Ahead

Abbie had always felt sorry for the spirits that Hurricane Katrina had disturbed so roughly and who were now doomed to wander forever in search of a decent pot of gumbo, not to mention a final resting place. She knew some of them had found their way to Atlanta. It was pretty obvious when the headless chickens started showing up, lying in a pathetic heap of shiny, blue black feathers at the crossroads of two wholly innocuous southwest Atlanta streets along with the first wave of displaced New Orleanians.

Around the same time, a tiny, dimly lit candle shop opened on the outskirts of West End, carrying everything from black cat bones and High John the Conquerer incense to a dizzying array of roots, herbs, and various potions guaranteed to get the job done, whatever that job happened to be. There had even been a few reports of headless goat carcasses showing up in city parks, but *vampires*? That was something else altogether.

Standing at the kitchen sink in the small apartment that had been her first home in Atlanta, and that she now maintained as a kind of informal West End Women's Center, Abbie felt nervous in a way she never had before. She hardly noticed the colorful bunch of flowers she was carefully arranging in a big, blue vase that matched the color of the walls in "the ocean room," as she called it, at the front of the apartment. She was glad Blue was on his way over to tell her what was going on.

She took a deep breath and headed back down the hall. Abbie placed the vase carefully on a table in the center of the sunny ocean room, and sank down gracefully on one of the deep purple meditation cushions that made this space a favorite among the women who came to her seeking solace or enlightenment or both. She loved this room, painted floor to ceiling in the most beautiful shades of blue, from turquoise to navy to the palest gray with touches of just-before-dawn pink. She had told Aretha that she wanted it to feel like the ocean and that's exactly how Aretha had painted it.

Abbie closed her eyes and took another deep breath to calm herself. She was surprised she hadn't picked up some kind of disturbance in the air indicating the presence of something as unnatural as vampires, but why would she? They weren't the same at all. She and Blue liked to call themselves *reincarnates*. They had died and returned many times, but there was no real connection between them and these strange creatures who never died and, according to Blue, never cracked a smile.

That would be awful, she thought, to live forever without any possibility of laughter. Abbie loved a good laugh. One of the things that had drawn her to Peachy Nolan and kept her by his side for the last four years was his sense of humor. The sex was great and the company was terrific, but the glue that held them together was their laughter. They laughed when they cooked, when they made love, when they watched the sunset, or toasted their good luck in finding each other. What if she'd been a vampire and missed all that? Abbie wondered, and she shivered a little.

At sixty-five *plus,* Abbie was in her prime and she knew it. Fit enough to turn cartwheels on her favorite Tybee Island beach whenever the spirit moved her, she had greeted the first signs of approaching menopause with the confusion and dread that seemed to be expected of women. But she had emerged on the other side, with determination and deep trust in the wisdom of her own natural femaleness, a self-described visionary, vital and invigorated, who could not only look deeply into her own heart and soul, but could help others navigate that often unknown territory as well.

She had been wrapping this new role around herself as if it were a gossamer shawl when Regina had emerged from a disastrous love affair, shell-shocked and shaken to the core. Abbie eagerly embraced the opportunity to bring her new gift of wisdom to bear on the life of her favorite niece, and they both emerged stronger from the collaboration. Soon after she had predicted that Regina would meet Blue in Atlanta, Abbie met Peachy at their engagement party and the two had been inseparable ever since.

Peachy had a house in Savannah that he had shared for twenty years with his late wife, and they both had carte blanche at Blue and Regina's Tybee Island beach house. The four of them regularly gathered there, with Sweetie in tow, begging her father to build her a sand castle. Two years ago, Peachy had opened a small restaurant on the island, called it Sweet Abbie's, found an amazing chef in Louie Baptiste, formerly of New Orleans, and now had so many customers that you needed reservations even during the off-season.

Abbie's work often kept her in the city, but Peachy shared her love of their independent lives, as much as they cherished their time together, and both were thriving. When Blue called, she told him she was driving down to Tybee that afternoon, but when he told her what was going on, she agreed to meet him immediately.

When he arrived a half an hour later, she had calmed herself and greeted him with an affectionate hug. "You okay?"

"Absolutely," he said.

"And how's your beautiful daughter?"

He smiled and nodded as she closed the door behind him. "Fine."

"Gina?"

"Fine, too. She's out with Aretha on the shoot."

"Does she know?"

Blue shook his head. "Not yet."

He followed her into the living room furnished simply in white wicker with lots of bright pillows. The white walls were unadorned by design, since Abbie felt that a person could more easily access her own dreams and visions without the presence of paintings, posters, or other artwork. Although it looked a little bare at first, its very neutrality was somehow more soothing than the dramatic walls of the ocean room.

Blue liked this room and they often talked here as confidants. When Regina first brought Blue home to meet Abbie, they had greeted each other like old friends, and so they were. She took a seat in a small rocking chair. Blue sat down on the love seat and placed his hat beside him.

"Aretha doesn't know either?"

"Neither one has any idea."

Abbie had so many questions, she didn't know where to begin. "Are you sure?"

"I'm positive," he said. "One of them came by the West End News. When I confronted her, she admitted it."

"How did you know?"

"I'm not sure," he said slowly. "I must have run across them before, but I can't remember when. There isn't any doubt in my mind, though. These women are the real thing."

"Are they dangerous?"

"Not anymore. Seems they've been able to substitute tomato juice to quiet any problematic cravings."

"*Tomato juice?*" Abbie sounded as incredulous as Blue had been when Serena first said it to him a few hours ago.

He nodded. "I know. It sounds crazy, but she seemed to be on the level."

"Can you read her clearly?"

One of Blue's gifts was a talent for mind reading, but a small frown flickered across his handsome face. His eyes, which changed colors as often as his mood, were now a deep gray. "Not as clearly as I'd like to. I knew what she was, but I can't seem to access what they're really doing here."

"I thought they were doing a fashion shoot for *Essence*."

"That much is true," he said, leaning back and crossing his legs. "Regina negotiated the whole thing."

Abbie smiled a little at the pride in his voice despite the seriousness of the topic. "Based on what I've heard, she got a pretty good deal, too."

Blue smiled back, his square, white teeth almost as startling as his eyes in that Africa-dark face.

"Go on."

"They got here yesterday. Aretha had dinner with them last night, and first thing this morning the leader of the group shows up to pay her respects."

"Do you think she knew that you had been here before?"

He shrugged. "I don't know. She seemed surprised that I knew so much about her, but I can't be sure. Their faces don't show much emotion."

"What did she say when you told her you knew?"

"She said they were from New Orleans, like I told you, and that they weren't dangerous as long as they had access to tomato products."

That would never be a problem in West End, Abbie thought, where bountiful community gardens provided enough fresh tomatoes to supply every family and neighborhood restaurant with them, fresh or canned, all year round. She hoped they weren't here to buy up the tomato crop. Somehow she didn't think the Growers Association would like that one bit.

"So where'd they go when they left Louisiana?"

"Somebody bought them an island," Blue said, like that was something that happened every day.

"An island?" Abbie said, incredulous. "Where?"

"She didn't say, but there's nothing much on it, so they come to the mainland every so often to make some money and lay in supplies."

"Including tomatoes?"

Blue smiled a little and shook his head. "No. I think they grow their own tomatoes."

"Good. Anything else?"

"They'll be here a week or so and then they're flying to Paris for another shoot."

"Nice work if you can get it," Abbie said. "Do you believe her story?"

"I don't know yet," Blue said slowly. "I don't think they're dangerous, not now anyway, but I think there's more to them being here than a magazine spread."

Abbie thought so, too. "What are you going to do?"

"I need more information," Blue said. "That's why I wanted to catch you before you went down to Tybee."

"Do you want me to talk to Regina before I go?"

"No," he said quickly. "I'll talk to Regina when the time is right. I want you to talk to Louis Baptiste and see if you can find out anything about a family named Mayflower back in New Orleans. A big family, probably had a lot of beautiful daughters. The one who came to see me was named Serena, but she's traveling with five others and I think they may be related."

"You think they're sisters?"

Blue shrugged. "I don't know, but anything he can tell me would help. The sooner, the better. I want to stay one step ahead of them."

The urgency of his tone made her realize how serious he was taking this whole thing. She could tell he was trying as hard not to alarm her as he was trying to avoid spooking Regina and completely freaking out Aretha, but Abbie needed to know it all.

"You're not telling me everything," she said gently. "What else did Serena Mayflower have to say?"

She wanted to feel the name in her mouth. It felt fake, like an amateur actor's attempt at a stage name.

Blue chose his words carefully. "She said this was a moment when they had to adapt or die, and they knew it."

"Adapt how?"

Blue stood up and reached for his hat. "That, Miss Abbie, is what we have to find out."

At the door, he kissed her cheek and she promised to drive carefully.

"When will you be back?"

"Sunday afternoon," she said.

"Good." He nodded. "Then don't call me from the island. Until we know more about how they communicate, it's probably better to talk face-to-face."

"I'm sorry you and Regina can't ride down with me."

Blue touched her shoulder lightly as he started down the stairs, and his eyes twinkled slightly for the first time that day. "I am, too, but somebody's got to stick around here and keep an eye on these vamps."

Abbie watched him walk out the bright blue front door and found herself suddenly hoping Aretha's sources were correct about its power to ward off evil. At this moment, she felt like she needed all the help she could get.

Chapter Seven

A Fabulous Opportunity

Aretha was in a zone. When the models and their stylists were finally satisfied with clothes, hair, makeup, and overall ornamentation, the Too Fine Five made their way upstairs, walked out into the Friday morning sunshine, and struck a pose as effortlessly strange and graceful as waterbirds taking flight over the Okefenokee Swamp. The crowd of students and onlookers, which had grown now to about one hundred, let out a collective gasp and fell back, heads tilted upward, eyes glued.

Regina knew that Aretha had intended to start by posing them at the base of the two-story King sculpture out front, but like any good artist, she recognized an opportunity and she took it. Instructing the models to simply walk among the young men without making any contact with them resulted in a wonderful series of shots that fully exploited the contrast between the students and their very ordinary environment and these frizzy-haired Amazons who seemed to have wandered in from a planet even more bizarre than this one. Without touching a single person, the girls cut a wide swath through the adoring assemblage, leaving in their wake besotted admirers who never spoke a word.

Once again, Regina was struck by the silence surrounding the women. As she was watching from just across the narrow street, she could hear the soft click of Aretha's camera shutter and her almost whispered instructions.

"Yes. Stop there. More with your arms. Yes. Just like that."

If Aretha harbored any ill will toward them based on their being bad body-image role models, you couldn't tell. The models obeyed her commands while incorporating the unique gyrations that had first made them lust objects for these same hormone-stuffed guys who had now been literally struck dumb by the women's physical presence. They were close enough to touch, but not one boy lifted a hand in their direction. Most of them were too intimidated to even make eye contact.

Aretha was moving through and around the crowd, snapping pictures and murmuring encouragement. The models didn't need it. Their languid posing seemed to have a life of its own. When she stopped to change cameras, they stood where they were without changing expression.

The blanker the better, Regina thought. *And whose idea of beauty was that?*

"Do you follow high fashion?" Serena's voice at her elbow seemed to answer the question Regina had just asked herself. It was a phenomenon she was used to since her husband and her aunt were both inveterate mind readers, although she had made them promise not to do it without her permission. She had no such agreement with Serena.

"Not so much," Regina said.

"Then how do you come to be representing a fashion photographer?" Serena's head moved very slightly in Aretha's direction like a weather vane on a day without much wind.

"She needed some advice and I was in a position to give it to her. Our arrangement is still fairly informal."

"I see," Serena said. "So should I be talking to you about what we hope is a very exciting opportunity, or should I wait and talk to Aretha directly?"

Regina looked at Serena's smoothly unreadable face and was glad their first negotiation had been on the phone. Trying to read her emotions like Regina could with most people would only be distracting and, ultimately, useless. Serena's expression never changed. If Aretha was going to do business with these women, she still needed all the help she could get.

"You can talk to me."

"Good."

Regina and Serena watched Aretha across the street, checking the lighting for the next shot. The models watched her, too, offering no opinions, while the ever-busy stylists stood on tiptoe to touch up the blush on a sharp cheekbone or gently dab a bit of color on a pair of pouty lips, outlined in crimson.

"She's a natural," Serena said in her breathy half whisper.

Regina nodded without turning toward her. It was easier to talk to Serena when she couldn't see her. "Yes, she is."

"I hope you weren't offended by Scylla's abruptness," Serena said, not turning around either. "She's responsible for the other girls on the road and sometimes, they can be a real handful."

"Not at all," Regina said. "She was right. What I gave wasn't much of an answer to a very real question. I'm glad it gave us a chance to clarify things."

"I'm glad, too," Serena said, nodding slowly.

She's as blank as her sisters or cousins or whatever they are, Regina thought. *These girls take having a poker face to a whole other level.*

Aretha had isolated two of the models for some close-ups and while she worked, two of the others stood waiting nearby, looking bored and ignoring the boys still hovering at a respectful distance. But off to one side, Regina saw Scylla engaged in an unexpectedly lively-looking conversation with a smaller group of five or six students wearing dark suits, white shirts, and maroon ties. They were looking up at her and although Regina was too far away to see their expressions, their body language was that of supplicants rather than would-be suitors.

"We're hoping to talk Aretha into taking over the shoot for our new portfolio," Serena said, gazing down at Regina. "She's got something fresh and original that's exactly what we're looking for."

No way was Regina going to admit right off that she had no experience with the intricacies of arranging to shoot portfolios for high-end fashion models, so she just nodded. "That sounds like a great opportunity."

"It's a *fabulous* opportunity," Serena said. "There are photographers all over the world who would kill for this chance."

Unfortunately, Regina thought, *Aretha is not one of them.* She could only imagine how hard she'd have to lobby to even get her to consider another assignment with these strange creatures, but that was part of an agent's job, wasn't it? Making sure the artist took advantage of the good things that came her way? Reminding her that the important thing was to create a body of interesting work, not to stand or fall on any one thing?

"How big a job is that usually?" Regina said.

"The biggest." Serena raised her eyebrows slightly in an approximation of surprise. "Models spend their lives fitting into someone else's fantasies. Sometimes we find those fantasies interesting and sometimes they are beyond banal. The portfolio is the only place where we get to work with somebody whose vision *we* decide we want to bring to life."

Regina had a sudden thought that perhaps the way they looked today was just the uniform required for the work they did, like a firefighter, or a lab technician, or a ballet dancer. Maybe when they weren't working, they put their hair in a sloppy ponytail, grabbed an old pair of jeans, some ballet flats, and headed for the mall. It was an interesting notion, but they would still be ten feet tall and skinny as a rail, so how much passing for regular could they do, even if they wanted to?

"Scylla and I look at everybody's work and we wait for that moment when we are touched by the soul of the artist, by the life force behind the vision. When we saw Aretha's stripper series in New York, we knew she was the one to do the new pictures. The way she humanized those women really resonated with us."

Several years ago, Aretha had taken a series of portraits of some of the dancers at Montre's, a notorious strip club that used to sit across the street from the West End Mall. She took two shots of each woman. The first one, naked or in costume. The second one, in whatever clothes made the woman feel most like herself. She hung the portraits side by side for the exhibition and the contrast between the women they projected for the paying customers and the women they really were was startling. Just looking at them did more to break through the wall between the dancers and the other women in West End than any abstract discussion about the nature of the sex industry and the need for bonding across lines of race and class. The show was a hit and scored a New York gallery showing for Aretha, which is where Serena discovered her. It also launched the careers of several of the featured dancers who suddenly found they could negotiate a better deal for themselves than Montre's five-dollar lap dances.

"I'm sure she'd be interested in exploring the possibilities," Regina said, wishing she knew more specifically what an agent was supposed to do at a moment like this.

"We'll pay top dollar," Serena said, watching Aretha crouching on a low wall to get the angle she needed. The model who had been so furious about her hair was moving through a series of poses so slowly that it looked as if she were underwater.

Regina had no idea what top dollar might be, but she didn't think Joyce Ann and Sweetie's classes needed to worry about having enough computers for quite a while. *Maybe through high school.*

"We need to get it done fast because we've got a shoot for French

Vogue coming up, and if I show them the same old pictures, they'll offer me the same old money," Serena said, "and that will never do."

"I understand," Regina said, wishing the woman would crack a smile, even a little one, now and again. "I'll be happy to talk to Aretha and gauge her interest, then maybe the two of you can . . ."

Before she could finish the sentence, Regina heard raised female voices and turned to see what was going on. Four of the models were huddled in a nervous knot in the middle of the street, gazing in the direction of the towering King sculpture the way people do when they glance across a field and see a funnel cloud headed in their direction.

Scylla was standing in front of Aretha, her Jimmy Choos practically toe-to-toe with Aretha's Dr. Martens, which were not backing up one inch. Without consulting each other, Regina and Serena moved immediately in the direction of the confrontation. The still smiling sergeant was standing nearby, but making no move to get any closer.

"It's in the contract," Scylla was saying in a loud, indignant voice. "How can you not know that?"

Aretha managed to look the woman in the eye even though she was a good six inches shorter, if you counted that hair. "Choosing locations is my responsibility, not yours. The statue is the reason we're here at this location in the first place."

Behind Scylla, the other models rippled a little, as if the very idea made them feel skittish. It was almost as if they hadn't noticed that they had been moving around in Doctor King's shadow all morning.

"All right," Aretha said briskly, pointedly turning away from Scylla and back toward the others, her eye quickly finding the two she was looking for. "I need you two over there near the base. One on each side. Get close, but don't touch it yet."

Their increasingly obvious discomfort manifested in a collective step in the opposite direction. They weren't even looking at the statue anymore, and merely being in its presence seemed more than they could handle. The two stylists hovered nearby but didn't get too close, as if the group might bolt at any minute, endangering any who got in its way.

What the hell is going on? Regina thought, turning to Serena, but Serena was watching Scylla, who was clearly not used to being challenged, much less so casually defied.

"It's against our religion," she snapped. "Look it up!"

Aretha stopped on a dime and spun around. She was losing patience and once that happened, there was always the chance that she would pack up her cameras and walk. Promises of portfolios notwithstanding. "What do you mean? That's Doctor Martin Luther King Junior, not Jesus Christ! *How can you not know that?*"

"We're not allowed to worship *any* graven images and that"— Scylla waved her long fingers in the direction of the statue without looking directly at it—"is definitely a graven image."

"I'm not asking you to worship it," Aretha said. "I'm asking you to pose."

Regina took a step closer in order to join the conversation before things got completely out of hand. She had read the contract many times and knew there was no mention at all of any religious prohibitions on anything.

"There's nothing like that in there," she said to Scylla, wondering if she should be talking to Serena instead. "I have a copy with me if you want to take a look, but I can assure you—"

"Our religion is very important to us, Ms. Hargrove," Serena interrupted her smoothly, still looking at Scylla. "We don't like to talk about it much because some in the fashion world don't respect real devotion that actually circumscribes the movement of your life. They're afraid it will get in the way of the client's wishes."

"The client had nothing to do with picking this location," Aretha said. "It was my choice alone."

"Then it is to you that I should appeal," Serena said, still silky smooth and conciliatory, "for your understanding and for your tolerance. We lost so many traditions in the hurricane. Perhaps we do cling a little too hard to the few that still remain, but they're all we have left. Can you find it in your heart to indulge our dwindling little band of survivors?"

She's good, Regina thought. *No way Aretha could resist such an appeal.*

Aretha sighed, a small frown signaling her resignation to surrender. "Of course I respect your religious beliefs. I just wish someone had told me before I built a whole idea around Doctor King."

Above their heads, the sculpture loomed majestic and oblivious.

"Of course, I accept full responsibility for the confusion, and for asking you to change horses in midstream," Serena said. "But I think the question now is, how can we make this work?"

"We can use what we've got already with these random kids," Scylla said immediately as if Aretha was no longer in charge or even particularly relevant. "Then we can take these five over here and do some stuff inside." She pointed to the guys Regina had seen talking to Scylla earlier, and they shrank back as if hanging around with a bunch of supermodels was the last thing on their minds.

Aretha looked at Scylla for about ten seconds and then turned to Serena. "Let me explain something to you," she said, her voice calm but steely. "If you want to shoot this yourself, or find another photographer to shoot it, you can pay me for my time and be my guest. But if you want me to take these pictures, then I am in charge of the creative vision. This is not a collaboration."

Scylla curled her lip in an arrogant sneer, although Aretha never turned back in her direction to see it. "Is that right?"

Aretha's eyes remained fixed on Serena. "That's right."

Her words hung heavily in the air in the sudden silence. Over Aretha's shoulder, Serena made eye contact with Scylla and it was clear who was really in charge. Serena's nod was so slight as to be almost imperceptible, but it produced an immediate response.

"All right," Scylla said, sounding annoyed. "I was out of line, okay? As a creative person, I sometimes get a little carried away, but I understand the need for boundaries."

"That's what first days are for," Aretha said, all business again. "Finding boundaries."

She looked up at the statue one more time, talking almost to herself. "*So*, no posing anywhere near Doctor King. I got it, but I'm going to need to do some rethinking."

Serena was standing next to her, seemingly waiting for instructions. The power was back in the right hands.

"Why don't we do this?" Aretha said. "Since we've already stopped, let's take a break, then the girls can change for the next setup."

The four other models who had been listening quietly, standing so close together they appeared joined at the same bony hip, relaxed and headed back toward the building without so much as a backward glance at the remaining boys, who watched until they disappeared inside, sighed, and then focused any remaining longing on Serena and Scylla, who couldn't have cared less.

Scylla looked at Aretha like she had a few things still on her mind, but thought better of it and headed inside, too.

"Maybe you're right after all," Scylla said to Serena over her shoulder. "She's tougher than she looks."

When the big glass door closed behind the last of the Too Fine Five, Serena turned to Aretha.

"Congratulations."

"For what?" Aretha said. "You haven't seen any pictures yet."

"For holding your own with Scylla. Most people are intimidated by her."

"I survived my daughter's terrible twos," Aretha said, rummaging around in the bag slung over her shoulder as she headed back toward the truck to reorganize her equipment. "I don't scare easily."

Good for you, Regina thought. *Don't take any stuff off these girls. We're in charge in West End, and don't you forget it.*

"That's good to know," Serena said, falling into step beside her, "because I'd love to work with you again."

That was the last thing Aretha expected to hear. She wondered suddenly if that whole scene with Scylla had been some kind of test to see if she was tough enough for the big time. She didn't like those kinds of games, but if that's the best they got, she thought, I'm home free.

"What did you have in mind?"

"A big assignment," Serena said. "Artistic freedom. Creative control. Great money."

Aretha chuckled and pulled out another camera, peered through the viewfinder, and set it down close by. "You should cut that as a record. Make yourself a video. Get the girls to do a little dance. How could anybody resist?"

"Can you?"

Aretha stopped sorting through her equipment. "Are you about to make me a job offer, Ms. Mayflower? Because if you are, I'm kind of busy right now, so I think you should probably talk to my agent."

"I already have," Serena said. "Perhaps she can share some of the details with you while I go check on the girls."

"Absolutely," Regina said, smiling in spite of herself. "I'd be glad to."

"Good," Serena said, nodding at them both as she headed inside. "It's a pleasure watching you work, Ms. Hargrove."

"Thank you, Ms. Mayflower," Aretha said, sweet as pie, but when Serena was safely out of sight, Aretha turned to Regina and shook her head.

"You better hurry up if you're going to make me rich and fabulous because I am about to knock one of these Glamazons out before the day is over."

"You're already pretty fabulous," Regina said, "but you're about to be a whole lot richer."

Aretha snapped open one of her cases and pulled out her favorite Leica. "As long as I don't pose them in front of any graven images, right?"

"They want you to shoot all the photographs for their new portfolio."

Aretha's busy hands stopped all motion. "Are you kidding?"

Regina shook her head. "Serena's ready to make you an offer right now."

"That's crazy! I almost came to blows with her superstar and now she wants to make a deal?"

"Some artists need that kind of drama to do their best work." The comment sounded innocent enough, but Regina was *signifyin'* and they both knew it.

"Then I guess I need to get back to that work." Aretha grinned. "Since I've got to rethink the whole afternoon's shoot."

"Go! Be creative!" Regina said, shooing her away. "I will open formal negotiations and find out exactly what these girls have in mind."

"Thank you," Aretha said, looking around the area quickly to be sure she wasn't leaving anything behind. "I've got so much stuff! What I really need is an assistant!"

"Duly noted," Regina said. "I'll put it in the contract."

Aretha hoisted her camera bag and looked at her friend. "You're good at this, you know?"

"Getting better all the time," Regina said. "Getting better all the time."

Chapter Eight

Dinner Rush

The drive from Atlanta to Savannah was about four hours and then just a short hop across the causeway to Tybee Island, Georgia's best-kept beach secret. An island too small to support the rampant overdevelopment that had already destroyed so many coastal communities, Tybee had great restaurants, amazing white sand beaches, friendly full-time residents, and enough local traditions to keep the mix lively, perhaps the best known of which was the annual Beach Queen Pageant, a veritable who's who of the island's eccentrics and the best party of the year.

When Abbie first saw Blue's beach house, nestled behind a giant sand dune, the view it offered of the Atlantic literally took her breath away. She spent hours just sitting on the back deck at dawn or watching the sunset from the tiny widow's walk that was reachable only by crawling out the window. Getting up there always made her feel like a kid shinnying up a backyard tree to sneak in after curfew.

She spent hours exploring the island, jogging on the beach, searching the horizon with Blue's big binoculars for the first glimpse of the giant freighters, pulling into Savannah Harbor with their mysterious loads of cargo containers stacked high against the bright blue sky. She watched the tiny shrimp boats chugging out before dawn and delighted in the porpoises leaping and splashing solely for their own pleasure, but maybe for hers, too, Abbie thought.

She was a great believer in the sacred interconnectedness of all things in the complex, never-ending circle of birth, life, death, spirit. That's why the whole idea of vampires was hard for her to accept. They were the antithesis of everything she believed. The *undead*? That meant the circle stopped with them, and so did the possibility of continuous regeneration. No idea of God she embraced could account for the presence of such beings, but there they were, roaming around her own West End neighborhood, with nothing to keep them in check but Blue.

She wasn't sure exactly how she was going to ask Louie Baptiste if he'd known any beautiful vampires back before the water chased them out, like it did almost everything he held dear. She shivered again, realizing as she turned into the almost empty parking lot at Sweet Abbie's that she hadn't asked Blue if she should tell Peachy what was going on. Probably not, she decided, spotting Louie's perfectly restored 1967 Cadillac DeVille in the spot reserved for Chef Baptiste. The spot marked for Peachy Nolan was empty.

Abbie glanced at her watch as she pulled into the space next to Peachy's. It was a little after two and the place was closed until dinner started at five. She knew Peachy would be back from wherever he was shortly, so she switched off the motor and walked around to the back kitchen entrance. A young man in a white T-shirt and a big white apron, its strings double wrapped around his slender midsection, was standing several feet away from the door smoking a cigarette. When he saw Abbie, he dropped it to the ground and smashed the butt out with his heel. She recognized one of Peachy's part-time dishwashers, Johnny Asbury, a third-generation islander, struggling through his last year of high school to please his mother before he went to work on the family shrimp boat. Shrimping was the only job he'd ever wanted to do and everybody smoked on a shrimp boat.

"Sorry, Miss Abbie," he said, looking sheepish. "You know I'm trying to quit."

"The only way to quit is to quit," Abbie said. "Chef around?"

"Yes, ma'am. He's just starting things up for dinner."

"Thanks," she said, giving him a motherly smile as she ducked inside. "You keep trying, okay?"

"Yes, ma'am," he said, wondering if he had time to sneak one more before he had to get back to work.

The kitchen in Sweet Abbie's was a large, spotlessly clean room with high ceilings and enough gleaming state-of-the-art cooking equipment to make Martha Stewart green with envy. Peachy had invested a fortune in accoutrements before hiring Louie, who was a traditionalist, preferring to chop his onions by hand and gauge the doneness of the meat by examining the clarity of the juice that trickled out when the meat was pierced with a clean toothpick. Peachy didn't care. It didn't make any difference to him *how* Louie cooked as long as he cooked. How could it? The food that Sweet Abbie's customers enjoyed was so good that once they tasted it, they were hooked.

When she peeked through the round, portal-like window in one of the two swinging silver doors, she could see the kitchen staff already at work. Louie, in his chef's whites from head to toe, was standing at a huge butcher-block chopping board calmly dictating the evening's menu to his assistant, also in white, who took it all down with great seriousness. There was no printed menu at Sweet Abbie's. Each night's offerings depended solely on the catch of the day, the bounty of the harvest, and the mood of the chef, who was, as in every well-run kitchen, the king.

She watched as the assistant read the menu back to Louie's satisfaction and then headed over to a quiet corner to transfer it to the small chalkboards that the waitstaff carried until they memorized the night's offerings. Abbie took a deep breath and fixed her face into a neutral smile. Of course, she was worrying about the sudden appearance of vampires in her life, but Louie didn't have to know it. Not yet, anyway.

"Hey, everybody," she called, pushing open the door. "I'm looking for a good chef. Anybody around here know where I can find one?"

General laughter all around as Louie turned around so fast, his chef's hat trembled like a half-set bowl of Jell-O. His smile was so genuine, crinkling the corners of his eyes in such a delighted, friendly way, that she was grateful as always for his presence in her life.

"Not one who's for sale." He laughed, crossing the room in three giant steps to enfold her in a big bear hug, as the kitchen staff waved and greeted her. Peachy treated his employees with respect and fairness and there was rarely any turnover. She knew them all by name.

"Well, then," she said, returning Louie's hug and kissing his warm, smooth cheek. "I guess I'll just have to keep looking."

He leaned back and grinned at her as his staff went back to work like the well-oiled machine they were. "Miss Abbie, you are a sight for sore eyes. Where you been keeping yourself?"

"Didn't Peachy tell you? I had two big projects to finish up in town."

"He told me, but you stayed away so long, I started thinking maybe you had decided to brighten up some other parlors."

"Not a chance," she said, laughing. "You two are stuck with me."

"Good thing, too," he said, leading her over to his small cubicle in a sunny corner of the kitchen and taking a seat beside her. He had a small desk, two chairs, and a tiny shelf crammed with notebooks full of his father's recipes. Katrina had destroyed the restaurant that had been in his family for three generations and scattered his loyal clientele to the four winds, but nothing could diminish his joy in the loving preparation of food. He learned to cook almost as soon as he could stand on a chair beside his father at the kitchen table. One of his first jobs was to carefully stir together whatever ingredients his father tossed into a big wooden bowl without the aid of any measuring cup or set of spoons. Louie's father cooked with *handfuls* of cornmeal and *pinches* of salt. His roux, every Louisiana cook's magic ingredient, was the stuff of legend, as was his gumbo, made from a secret recipe that he passed on as a sacred trust to his son only once Louie had proven himself worthy, well into his twenties.

"Without you, we'd have to change the name of this place, like it or not, and you know how that can confuse people," Louie was still teasing. "Not to mention the effect your departure would have on Brother Nolan, who is already hanging on by a very slender thread."

"I doubt that."

"It's true, Miss Abbie," Louie protested. "When you're not on this island, he is just this side of pitiful. He stands in front of that picture up front and looks for all the world like a man about to die of a broken heart."

Abbie laughed. Their friendship was based on an easy foundation of gentle teasing and they both enjoyed it.

"Where is my true love, anyway?" Abbie said, looking around as if Peachy might be hiding behind a big bag of Vidalia onions or a giant sack of flour.

"Gone to see Mr. Chu about our liquor order," Louie said and rolled his eyes.

No surprise there, Abbie thought. Mr. Chu owned a number of businesses on the island, including a liquor distributorship, and he and Peachy were engaged in an endless series of discussions about pricing. Peachy claimed he was being cheated blind and Mr. Chu claimed he was being driven to the poorhouse by his efforts to be fair to his valued customers.

"He'll be back in a minute. You hungry?"

"I'm fine," Abbie said, realizing this was her chance to raise Blue's question with Louie before Peachy returned. "Actually, I was hoping to have a chance to talk with you alone."

Louie grinned at her. "Well, I won't tell if you don't."

"Fair enough," Abbie said, grinning back. "I just wanted to ask if you ever knew a family of Mayflowers back in Louisiana."

The smile froze on Louie's, face, but his voice was noncommittal. "Mayflower?"

"They may have had a lot of daughters."

Louie tugged at his chin like he was trying to remember. "Tall, skinny gals?"

"That's right. You know them?"

Louie fiddled with a tiny bottle of Tabasco sauce on his desk. Abbie wondered if the vampires were allowed to spice up their tomato juice with some hot sauce; maybe a shot of vodka every now and then.

"I heard of them. Everybody in Reserve know about the Mayflowers."

Reserve was Louie's tiny hometown, located right outside New Orleans.

The question is, Abbie thought, *what did they know?* "One of them came to see Blue this morning."

"In Atlanta?"

Abbie nodded.

"Came to see him about what?"

She looked at Louie for a minute and then did what she always did: went straight to the heart of the matter. "It's true, isn't it?"

Louie sighed and smoothed his hands over the spotless expanse of his apron. A few Christmases ago, he had given his friends black aprons that said, *Don't make me have to poison your food,* but this one was just plain.

"Miss Abbie, this is not something to be discussed in the middle of preparations for the Friday night dinner rush," he said gently.

"But is it true?"

"What did Blue say?"

"He's the one who wanted me to ask you about the Mayflowers."

"Then I'll tell you what I know, but not now. Tomorrow, after I pick the fish."

As serious as the topic under discussion was, Abbie had to smile. First and foremost, Louie Baptiste was a chef. Sweet Abbie's prided itself on serving the freshest seafood on the island. No way was Louie going to let some vampires get in the way of that hard-won distinction.

Abbie had no choice but to wait. The first seating for dinner was in three hours, and the kitchen was already coming alive around them as Louie's small staff moved about efficiently, communicating with a minimum of verbal exchanges, as longtime coworkers often do. They all knew what Friday nights were like, and that by six thirty a line of happy, hungry people would be halfway down the block. The best way to survive it with your sanity and your tips intact was to do your job and stay loose. Abbie knew the rules and she respected them.

"You're right," she said, standing up to leave him to his work. "I'll wait for Peachy out front. This is no time to talk."

"Tomorrow morning will be time enough," Louie said, standing up, too, and sounding relieved. She was his friend, but she was also the boss's wife and attention must be paid. "Nothing's going to happen between now and then."

"Like what?" Abbie said.

"Like nothing," he said, hoping he sounded reassuring as he walked her to the door. "The Mayflowers aren't dangerous anymore. If they were, don't you think Blue would have said so?"

"I know he would have," she said. She watched the sous chef carefully stirring a red sauce in a deep iron pot. The spicy smell of tomatoes and garlic made her stomach growl and she realized she was hungry after all.

"Then stop worrying," Louie said gently, opening the door slowly so she wouldn't think he was being rude. "Everything is fine."

Abbie stopped in the doorway and raised her eyebrows. "Is that why you're giving me the bum's rush?"

"Dinner rush, Miss Abbie. *Dinner rush.*"

"Just checking," she said, and heard her stomach growl again, this time so loudly that Louie heard it, too. He grinned.

"I know you're not hungry, but how about I send you out a cold chicken sandwich anyway? You can just pick at it until your man gets back."

"Bless you." Abbie laughed, heading down the short hallway to the restaurant's main dining room as Louie's assistant approached holding out a cellphone and looking concerned. "If things get crazy later, I'll just see you in the morning."

"I'll be there," he said as the door swung closed and he was gone.

Abbie liked being in the empty restaurant before it opened for dinner. It was like sitting in a church sanctuary before Sunday service. Peaceful, but in a nice, anticipatory kind of way. She stopped right inside the front door at the main entrance and there was the picture Louie had been teasing her about. It was a beautiful color portrait of Abbie by the ocean on a perfectly cloudless day. She looked happy and sexy and exactly like the kind of woman you'd want to have a nice long dinner with.

At Peachy's request, Aretha, who took the picture, had framed it in a heavy, old-fashioned gilt frame, like the kind that hangs over the bar in all those old Hollywood Westerns. Whenever she came to the restaurant, people got very excited and asked her to pose with them in front of it. She always agreed, smiling pleasantly as they embraced her shoulders awkwardly or pointed up at the portrait, as if anyone could somehow miss the fact that it was her smiling down at them.

She liked that picture. Aretha had taken it only a few weeks after Abbie realized she was falling in love with Peachy. The idea that he liked it so much that he stood before it, feeling such longing that his suffering was visible to the naked eye, filled her with deep pleasure. Louie was right. There was enough time tomorrow to figure out the Mayflowers. She hadn't seen Peachy in almost two weeks and she missed him like crazy.

Tonight, she thought, smiling back at her own image, *all you need is love. And maybe a nice cold chicken sandwich.*

Chapter Nine

Something Very Strange

It had been a very busy day. Since he first arrived at eight o'clock and found Serena Mayflower waiting in his office to the last phone call from his friend Noel in Trinidad that had just ended a few minutes before seven, Blue Hamilton had been wearing with equal aplomb the many hats required of him in the course of an average twenty-four-hour day.

Blue had made his artistic reputation as a singer, but he had made his fortune in real estate. Although he was known for his extensive commercial and residential properties throughout West End, Blue's holdings went far beyond the boundaries of the small southwest Atlanta community where he had chosen to live and work. Recent developments in world markets had tripled the value of his partnership with a Trinidadian songwriter turned oilman who had a line to Venezuelan president Hugo Chávez. Blue's friend also held the distinction of having penned more number one hits than anyone else in the history of Carnival, including the collaboration that rocked the island several years earlier when Blue came briefly out of retirement to lend his unique vocals to the project and render the song an instant classic.

Noel was begging Blue to come back and do it one more time, but so far there were no real plans to make it happen. Blue and Regina had spent almost a year in Trinidad when Sweetie was just learning to walk. Going back was a dream they often whispered about, lying in each other's arms, remembering how sweet it had been to make love listening to the sound of the ocean outside their window.

"Soon come," Blue always said, in the island patois that meant twenty minutes or twenty years, depending on whom you asked. "Soon come."

He couldn't deny that there had been something very appealing about stepping back from all of his West End responsibilities. His financial holdings were easily managed electronically, with minimal face-to-face contact required, but his actual presence in and around this neighborhood was an absolute necessity. Blue's ability to hold things together was based in part on his well-known willingness to do whatever needed to be done to maintain the overall peace, but it was also the result of his undeniable personal charisma. As a singer, the power of that charisma had made grown women weak in the knees. In his current role, it sometimes did the same to grown men.

Blue had thought once that the neighborhoods that bordered West End on every side would be transformed by their proximity to the twenty or so square blocks where he was in charge. He had hoped, and he had worked and he had waited, but not only had there been no positive change, many of the neighborhoods were actually getting worse. Unemployment was rampant. Drug addiction was epidemic. And maybe most surprising to Blue was that the election of a young black president who wanted to change the world and needed all the help he could get seemed to make little lasting impact among the young brown men he saw every day who wore their pants below their butts and had no larger vision than controlling the sale of crack cocaine in a half-block radius. It also made no difference at all to the young brown women whose children's lives were already set in motion before their first birthdays to repeat every negative pattern. After years of sustained effort, Blue was beginning to suspect that there wasn't a damn thing he could do about any of it beyond this tiny community where he had drawn a line that didn't move.

Through the smoked glass, Blue saw Henry coming down the hall. He stopped and spoke a few words to Jake and then tapped on Blue's door twice like he did every night at precisely seven fifteen.

"Come ahead," Blue said.

Henry stepped into the room, graceful for a man his size, and closed the door behind him.

The two men sat together for a few minutes every evening to review the events of the day and get ready for the next one. To describe Henry as Blue's right-hand man was to not recognize the multifaceted nature of his role. Each man trusted the other with his life, and constant, truthful communication was a necessity.

Blue nodded slightly. "Want a drink?"

"Absolutely," Henry said.

Neither man loosened a tie or removed a jacket.

"Why don't you do the honors?"

Henry poured them each a generous splash of cognac and carefully replaced the cork. He walked back to his seat and handed Blue a snifter before taking his usual seat across from Blue.

"Anything happening I need to know about?" Blue said.

"Everything is everything," Henry said, sounding like an old-school jazz musician. "I took care of that thing we talked about this afternoon and the team we sent over to Morehouse said they're done for the day. Five of the models went back to their hotel and the one who was here earlier went over to Brandi's with Aretha Hargrove. They're having drinks right now. Your wife picked up your daughter and Joyce Ann Hargrove and took them both to your house."

"Any problems over there today?"

Henry shook his head. "None at all. Was there anything specific you were expecting?"

"No," Blue said, wondering when *was* the right time to warn your closest associates that there were vampires in their midst. "But we never want to be careless."

Henry took a swallow of his drink and set it down slowly on the table in front of him. "I'm not exactly sure how I should say this."

Blue looked at Henry, his eyes giving off no light and his expression neutral.

"Just say it," Blue said. "What's on your mind?"

"That woman who came by this morning?"

"Ms. Mayflower?"

"Yes, Ms. Mayflower. I was just wondering if you noticed anything *strange* about her."

"Other than the fact that she's probably the tallest, thinnest woman either one of us has ever seen?" Blue smiled, waiting for the next question.

"You got that right," Henry said, and Blue could see him relax a little. "But that's not what I meant entirely."

Blue knew that it was time to tell Henry. *Past* time. How could he expect the man to protect him if he didn't even know what the danger was?

"I know what you mean," Blue said. "There is something very strange about Serena Mayflower and I want your solemn vow that when I tell you what it is, that information will not leave this room."

Henry leaned forward and clasped his big hands on the table. They looked even bigger against the starched white cloth. "Mr. Hamilton, you have my word."

"Good. And do me a favor?"

"Yes?"

"Call me Blue."

Chapter Ten

The Senior Princess

Regina didn't know who was more excited. Aretha making her way down I-20 to share the good news or the two little girls upstairs, wriggling into their princess outfits for a trip to the mall for ice cream. It was probably a tie, although she doubted that Aretha could compete when it came to high-pitched squealing. The truth was Regina was excited, too. The rest of the first day's shoot had gone so well, it was almost as if the morning face-off between Scylla and Aretha had never happened.

After the models had lunch, or whatever they did in place of eating, they reported back to Aretha with a new set of outfits—again having no resemblance to the wardrobe of any college professor who had ever earned a living on planet Earth—and a willingness to pose all over the campus without complaint. Everywhere they went, they attracted adoring groups of students who always got in the shoot if they were invited, but otherwise hung back at a respectful distance, content to say they had been in the presence of a phenomenon without actually having to engage with it.

The ease of interaction between Aretha and the models allowed Serena and Regina to stand off to one side and informally discuss the details of the portfolio assignment throughout the afternoon. By the end of the day, Regina had received an offer larger than Aretha could ever have imagined, a promise of complete creative control, *and* an assistant.

Serena had emphasized again and again that they never presented themselves in a traditional style. Their portfolios were always art projects as well as marketing tools.

"It's her vision we want," Serena said. "First and foremost, she's an artist."

And after this assignment, a very well-paid artist, Regina thought, stacking the last of the dishes in the sink and going to the foot of the stairs to check on the princesses.

"Anybody need any help up there?"

Her daughter popped out of her bedroom door and into the hallway. At four years old, Sweetie had her mother's bright smile and her father's amazing blue eyes. She was wearing a frilly, pink princess dress and a golden crown balanced delicately on top of her head right between her old-school Afro puffs.

"We're coming, Mommy," she said. "We have to find one to fit Joyce Ann."

At six, Joyce Ann had already outgrown most of these pastel confections and passed them on to Sweetie, but Regina had said they could dress up for a trip to the Baskin-Robbins if they ate all their vegetables at dinner, so they were happy to improvise.

"Try the white one with the wings," Regina said, forgetting which character the outfit represented. "I think it's a little longer than the others."

"Okay, Mommy," Sweetie said, and disappeared into what Regina knew was a cloud of scratchy net and pseudo-satin costumes flung everywhere in an effort to find one that did justice to Joyce Ann's rank as the senior princess.

There was no reason to rush them. Aretha was on her way, but she was coming from midtown, so it would be another fifteen minutes before she'd burst in with the details of her dinner with Serena. She was too excited to talk and drive, so Regina had no choice but to wait for some specifics. When Serena first extended the dinner invitation, Aretha had declined since it was already after five o'clock and she was just packing up the truck. She had to pick up her daughter by six. But Regina jumped in without hesitation, offering to pick up Joyce Ann and take her home with Sweetie, where Aretha could pick her up later.

Serena had said time was of the essence, and as far as Regina was concerned, all that remained before they could seal the deal and sign on that very lucrative dotted line was to see if Aretha and Serena could work together—as members of the same creative team. Aretha was a lone wolf and Serena was an alpha bitch if she had ever seen one, Regina thought, smiling at the canine images that popped into her mind. If those two could figure out a way to work together, she had no doubt the pictures would be amazing. If they couldn't, there was no need to belabor the process. They could finish up this shoot for *Essence* and call it a day, but Aretha hadn't sounded like a woman about to call anything a day. She sounded like a woman who had just glimpsed a whole new set of possibilities.

Regina glanced at her watch. It was almost eight and she knew Blue would be home any minute. She headed for the front door to turn on the porch light just in time to see the big black Lincoln pull up to the curb in front of their house. Upstairs, she could hear the princesses gathering their scepters and amping up the squeal factor.

"Daddy's home!"

Chapter Eleven

The Surprise Factor

Regina opened the door and Blue saw, framed in the light, his daughter and Joyce Ann in full princess regalia—one pink, one white with wings—waving like mad. Just behind them, his wife was wearing her best "Welcome home, baby" smile. It was one of his favorite moments of the day, but tonight he felt the smallest twinge of guilt.

Blue wasn't accustomed to hiding things from Regina, but now he had told two people about the vamps, and she was still standing in the doorway, smiling and waving, completely oblivious. He had to tell her, no matter what her reaction might be. He owed her that much. Henry had taken it really well, Blue thought. He seemed surprised—who wouldn't be?—but he didn't freak out. He had listened to what Blue had to say, taken a big swallow of his cognac, and asked for instructions.

"For right now, all we want to do is keep an eye on them," Blue had told him. "When we have more information, we'll know whether or not we need to make a move."

"I'll be ready," Henry had said quietly. "You just say the word."

Blue had wished he could just say the word, but that would mean he had decided on a course of action, an appropriate response, and the truth was, he hadn't. Not yet. That was no excuse, of course. He hadn't promised Regina infallibility. He had promised her the truth. Withholding it, for whatever laudable reason, was just another form of lying, and he knew it.

The princesses were already hopping up and down as Blue headed up the walk to greet them.

"Daddy, we're going for ice cream! Can you come, too?"

"I don't think so, darlin'," Blue said, leaning down to kiss her cheek. "How you doin', Miss Joyce Ann?"

"I'm fine," she said, taking the hand Sweetie wasn't already clutching. "I don't have the right shoes because I didn't know we were going to dress up, but you can hardly tell, can you?"

"Never noticed it at all," Blue said, leaning forward to accept Regina's kiss. She hugged him briefly around the neck and he grinned, prevented by the princesses hanging at the end of each arm from hugging her back.

"Where's your princess dress?"

"They didn't have one to fit me!" she said, laughing.

He raised his eyebrows, his eyes glowing softly in the hall light. "Well, we'll have to work on that."

"Work on what, Daddy?"

Sweetie was skipping along happily by her father's side and he was reaching to close the door and answer the question when Joyce Ann dropped his hand. "There's my mom!"

The happy announcement brought both princesses back outside to repeat their welcome wave for Aretha's arrival.

"Mommy!" Joyce Ann called, wanting to share the good news first. "We're going to get ice cream! Can you come with us?"

Aretha practically skipped up the front steps. "Not only will I come, it will be my treat!"

The girls released Blue's hands without a backward glance and danced around Aretha, their new best friend. Blue laughed, immediately reaching out a free hand to encircle Regina's waist and pull her close as they all headed back inside. "I guess that shows me who my real friends are!"

"Don't worry," Aretha said, twirling the princesses effortlessly around as she spoke. "With all the money Regina and I are going to be making, we'll buy you some new friends."

Joyce Ann frowned. "You can't buy people, Mommy!" she said, sounding concerned.

Aretha laughed. "Oh, no, baby! Of course you can't!" And she leaned down to pat her daughter's cheek. "Mommy was just acting silly."

"Can we go now?" Sweetie said, gazing up at Aretha with a look of such hopeful anticipation that Regina laughed.

"We're going, Sweetie," she said. "You two go upstairs first and get your sweaters and put on some socks. It's a little cool out there."

The two walked upstairs slowly, holding their dresses out before them carefully to avoid catching a toe in the fragile, flame-retardant fabric and ripping the skirt off at the waistband. After such a disaster, the skirt would never hang right again, no matter how many attempts were made to repair it. This was a tragedy with which both princesses were familiar and they were not eager to relive it any time soon.

"Look at them." Aretha shook her head. "We might as well bind their feet!"

"But not tonight," Regina said quickly. "At least not until you tell me how it went with Serena."

Blue felt a little shiver of discomfort. He wished these vamps would hurry up and finish with their Atlanta business and get out of town. They made him feel uneasy and he didn't like it one bit.

Aretha grinned. "You are a genius. It's definitely a go!"

Now it was Regina's turn to let out a high-pitched squeal. "You're sure?"

"I'm positive! I have officially sold my soul to the devil!"

Then they both started hugging each other and jumping around in the middle of the front hallway like two maniacs. Blue waited for them to remember that because of Regina's prohibition on unsolicited mind reading, he had no idea what exactly they were celebrating.

"She said you two can work out the final agreement over the weekend, we'll finish the shoot on Monday, and start storyboarding the new piece on Monday."

Regina raised her eyebrows. "Storyboarding?"

"I told her I wanted to think of it like a film," Aretha said, turning to Blue excitedly. Her long silver earrings were bobbing around like they were excited, too. "I'm going to storyboard the whole thing before we shoot a single scene. I don't want any repetition of that craziness outside the chapel this morning."

"Sounds great," Blue said, wondering what craziness, "but I'd probably enjoy it a whole lot more if I knew what we were celebrating."

"Oh, Lord," Regina said, laughing apologetically. "I didn't even have a chance to tell you the good news."

"Drumroll, please!" Aretha said.

"Our favorite photographer . . ."

"Yours truly . . ."

"Has just received a huge new assignment and an obscenely large commission to create a brand-new portfolio for the hottest group of models in the world today."

Blue willed his eyes to remain impassive and fixed his smile in place to hide his surprise, but not before Regina saw the flash of annoyance—or was it something else?—flicker across his face.

"The ones you're shooting for *Essence*?"

"Those are the very ones," Aretha said happily. "Weirdest bunch of women I've ever seen, but I have to admit, the challenge of shooting them on my own terms, without the need for all that high-fashion hoopla, does appeal to me. Plus, the money is insane. I may never have to throw myself on your tender mercies again!"

"When did all this happen?"

"Ask your amazing wife," Aretha said, draping her arm around Regina's shoulders. "While we were shooting, she was making Ms. Mayflower give up the goods *big time*. She's a natural-born agent. Just ask her!"

"So you've been out doing deals behind my back," Blue said, teasing her gently.

"This is my first," Regina said, "but if it's always this easy, I'm hooked."

"Me, too," said Aretha. "I'm going to pay off all my student loans, every credit card I owe, pay Joyce Ann's tuition, and still be able to buy that Leica I've been lusting after for two years. It's amazing!"

"Did she smile when you told her you'd do it?"

"Fat chance," Aretha said. "I don't think they have it in them."

"You should see these women," Regina said to Blue. "They never change expressions."

"I know," he said. "I met one this morning."

Regina was surprised. "You did? Which one?"

"Serena Mayflower. She came to pay her respects since they were going to be working in West End for a few days."

"I told her it was customary to check in with the godfather," Aretha said, as Joyce Ann appeared in the upstairs hallway.

"Auntie Gina, I can't find my sweater."

"It's probably buried under all those costumes they tried on," Regina said. "Hang on a second."

But Aretha reached out a hand to stop her. "I got this. See if you can talk your handsome husband into coming out to celebrate with us." She took the steps two at a time and disappeared into Sweetie's room.

Regina turned to Blue. "You didn't tell me you met Serena Mayflower."

He smiled. "I just walked in, remember?"

He was right, but Regina was still looking at him like any loving wife looks at her loving husband when she stumbles upon something in conversation that she feels like she should already have known. The specific information didn't really matter. It was the surprise factor that gave her pause. That and the fact that Serena hadn't mentioned it, either.

"What did you think of her?" Regina's tone wasn't nearly as neutral as she hoped it would be.

Blue could hear Sweetie and Joyce Ann making their final wardrobe decisions with Aretha, and he knew it would be only a minute before they would all come down, demanding milk shakes and double-dip, mint chocolate chip ice cream cones. There was no time to go into what he thought and what he knew about Serena Mayflower.

He smiled at Regina and reached up to loosen his tie. "I thought she could use a little more meat on her bones. Didn't you?"

"Of course I did." Regina relaxed a little and walked over to him close enough to rest her hands against his chest. "But spending the day around a bunch of women who get paid for being beautiful can take its toll on an ordinary woman's self-esteem."

"Well," he said slowly, resting his hand on her behind lightly, "since you are an extraordinary woman, that shouldn't be a problem."

"Good answer, Mr. Hamilton," she said. "And for that, you do not have to join us at the Baskin-Robbins, but promise me one thing."

"Anything," he said, as their daughter started her descent, gown carefully bundled under one arm while the other hand clutched the banister.

"Here we come, Daddy!"

And an echo from Joyce Ann, holding on tight to her mother's hand. "Here we come!"

"What's the promise?" Blue said.

Regina smiled and kissed her husband's cheek. "Wait up for me so you can tell me again how much you like a woman with a little meat on her bones," she whispered.

"You got it," he said, turning to Sweetie, who was about halfway down the stairs, getting tangled up in her dress in her eagerness to reach her father.

"Here I come, Daddy!"

Blue held out his arms. "Jump, baby!"

She looked at him, her eyes big blue Os of surprise. Sweetie was not allowed to play on the stairs, but this was her daddy giving her an order. That made it different. She hesitated, and then met his grin with her own. "For real?"

He nodded. "Jump!"

And with a squeal of delight, she launched herself off the steps and hurtled fearlessly into her father's open arms. Joyce Ann and Aretha applauded, laughing. Regina did, too, but watching her husband over their daughter's head, she couldn't help but wonder what else he hadn't told her.

Chapter Twelve

New Orleans Sob Story

When Serena opened the door of their suite, she found her second-in-command curled up in the corner of a big white couch, wrapped from neck to knee in the hotel's fluffy white terry-cloth robe, drinking a glass of red wine, and gazing intently at the big flat-screen television. She had washed the high-fashion frizz out of her hair, tucked the damp strands behind her ears, and scrubbed the bilious green paint off her eyelids, but she still looked like she had dropped in from another planet.

"Everything okay?" Scylla said, without taking her eyes off the screen where she was clicking through the options.

Serena closed the door, hung her coat in the closet, and stepped out of her stilettos. "Everything's fine."

"Good."

Serena glanced out the window at the full moon hanging heavy and golden and then headed to the minibar. The view from the four-teenth floor was beautiful but not distractingly so. They weren't up high enough for breathtaking.

"Want a drink?" she said, reaching for the Bloody Mary mix and a couple of tiny bottles of Absolut.

Scylla drained her wineglass and set it down carefully on the end table beside her.

"I'll take that as a yes," Serena said.

Scylla watched her empty the vodka into the mixer and stir both glasses delicately with a swizzle stick. "I wish we could go back to the good old days when we could end the evening with a nice Caber-net. Tomato juice? *Please!*"

"You know we developed an immunity to it after all those years." Serena carried both glasses across the room and set one down in front of Scylla. "Red wine doesn't do it anymore, so just relax and enjoy."

Scylla shook her head and held up a slender hand in mock protest. "You put vodka in it. Too many calories!"

From where she had taken a seat at the other end of the couch, Serena turned slowly to face her friend.

"Just kidding," Scylla said, making the strange little hissing sound that indicated they were amused. Without the ability to smile, laugh-ing was out of the question. "Can you imagine having to actually *think* about being thin. What a waste of time!"

She took a big swallow of her drink, more to please Serena than from any desire for more tomato juice, still clicking aimlessly through the channels the hotel provided. Sports, movies, kid cartoons, finan-cial news in Japanese, weather, more sports, adult cartoons, sitcoms, local happenings, and, for a few extra bucks, all the porn you could handle.

"You were good, today," Serena said. "You did a wonderful job getting the girls ready."

"I'll admit, it was harder than I thought it would be," Scylla said.

"If they hadn't decided to start breeding for brains pretty soon, there is a real risk of our little tribe introducing something never before seen in all of recorded history."

"What's that?"

"A dumb vampire."

They hissed softly again at the very idea. Vampires prided themselves on being strong *and* smart.

"You were good, too," Scylla said. "That New Orleans sob story always gets them. I don't see how you can even say that shit."

"It's true!"

Another low hiss. "Please! You make us sound like a bunch of nuns or something. I've heard you. 'We lived in peace with the locals there for generations.' Sure we did. As long as they didn't poke their noses in where they had no business."

"Well, whatever we were, we still lost everything we had, didn't we?"

"Yeah, so?"

"So nothing. We're here to fulfill our mission and that's what we're going to do. A few more weeks and we'll be on our way home and your good nature can return at last."

Scylla groaned and tossed the remote control down on the couch between them. "I'm so bored! Why the hell are you dragging things out like this? It's bad enough in New York and L.A., but these hicks are just ridiculous."

"Their contract says they have ten days after their due date to bring their witnesses forward and plead their case. They've got one more week."

"Like anybody cares."

Serena didn't want to argue. She picked up the remote and continued clicking, but nothing caught her eye. Insomnia was practically part of their DNA, so she knew they would be up for a while. Too bad she'd seen every movie they were offering and none of them were good enough for repeated viewings.

"I'm sorry, but did you see our guys over at Morehouse today?"

Scylla said, still sounding annoyed. "They were totally freaking out, with their little blue jackets and maroon ties. Did they think we'd be impressed with that boarding school getup?"

"They're children," Serena said. "What did you expect?"

"They're twenty-one! When do we get to start calling them men?"

"When they do."

Scylla sighed. "You ever think maybe we'd be better off without them?"

"I always think we'd be better off without them, but until you have a viable alternative, the question is moot."

"We're wasting time with all this recruiting and drawing up contracts and paying off potential witnesses." Scylla rippled her arms in mild agitation. "I think we should just swoop in there, grab the ones we want, and take them home with us. End of story."

"It's rape if you just snatch the ones you want," Serena said calmly. "We can't jump-start our gene pool by raping people."

"Even if it's a matter of survival?"

"No rape." Serena stopped briefly on a video of Michael Jackson in full crotch-grabbing mode, but changed the channel quickly. Even though people sometimes speculated that he might be one of theirs, she knew better.

Scylla shook her head. "That's why women's cultures always die out, because we're always so goddamn concerned about being good little girls."

"Women's cultures die out because we can't find a way to reproduce without men," Serena said calmly.

Scylla stretched her long arms over her head and sighed. "If you cared anything about money, I'd bet you a million dollars not one of those little punks could get his own grandmother to say *Spare this chile!*"

"Well, the good thing is the portfolio shoot gives us a reason to hang around and keep an eye on them without arousing any suspicion in Mr. Hamilton."

"Why should he care? From what I understand, the college guys don't have much to do with the people who live in West End anyway."

"That may be true, but Blue Hamilton doesn't strike me as the kind of man who would take kindly to anything *untoward* happening in his own backyard."

"Even if his wife stands to make a sizable commission on the deal?"

"Don't kid yourself. He doesn't care about money any more than I do."

"I know that, but still . . . *Oh! Stop! Serena, stop!*" Scylla was on her feet waving her hand at the television excitedly. "That's it! That's the movie I've been telling you about. The one where Thandie Newton does our dance. *Watch!* It's coming up right now!"

Serena did as she was told, glad for a reason to change the subject. She needed more information before offering a definitive opinion on Mr. Hamilton.

"That's Gerard Butler," Scylla whispered as he began to dance in front of Thandie Newton, who was seated on a low settee at some kind of very cool party, smoking one of those long thin cigarettes that mysterious, multiracial women at very cool parties always smoke in Guy Ritchie movies. When he asks her to dance, she looks at him and then stands up slowly, or rather sort of unfolds in front of him.

"Watch her now!" Scylla whispered urgently, as if Serena's attention might wander at the crucial moment. *"Watch her!"*

As soon as she started to move, Serena immediately understood Scylla's excitement. The actress was doing their signature dance like she had been born for it. Thandie had taken as her own the almost graceful, almost herky-jerky, undeniably strange, somewhat spidery, often slithery, always sexy thing that had made them famous, and she was *doin' it to death,* the highest compliment a vampire could offer.

"I can't believe it," Serena said admiringly. "She's amazing."

"I told you," Scylla said. "Is that our shit or what?"

"It's absolutely *our shit*," Serena said, although she usually didn't curse. "No question."

"Did you know she was . . ."

Serena shook her head quickly. "She's not one of us. Maybe she's just . . . maybe she's just really a great dancer."

"You got that right! Look at her go!"

Thandie slithered over closer to her partner, who was trying to figure out if it was possible to have sex with this strangely gyrating, birdlike creature, or if this was as close as he was going to get. Scylla and Serena, both standing now, moved a little closer to the television and began to sway in unison just like they had done in the video that catapulted them to the top of the pop heap. Their movements mirrored Thandie's without the two even consulting each other, so that the three women seemed to be doing the same choreography.

"So you don't care about money, huh?" Scylla said, without taking her eyes off the actors.

"No." Serena didn't look away either.

On the screen, Thandie turned her back to Gerard and shook her tiny little ass in his direction.

"So what do you care about?"

Serena stopped moving and looked at Scylla, who stopped right with her. "Nothing," she said softly. "Not a damn thing."

"Good," Scylla said as they started moving again. "Just checking."

Chapter Thirteen

What She Had to Say

Saturday

It was not unusual for Abbie to leave Peachy sleeping and come up to the small deck at the top of the house to watch the sun rise. She would curl up in one of the rockers, pull her shawl around her, and clear her mind for the day ahead. She loved to watch the dark sky gradually turn from gray to peach to palest blue, all in anticipation of the sun, rising up out of the water bright and majestic on some days, and on others, hidden behind clouds that seemed to blend with the water into one unbroken canvas of mist and mystery.

It was that kind of moist morning and Abbie pulled her shawl a little tighter. It had been a lovely night. Peachy had filled the house with flowers and candles, chilled a bottle of French champagne, and cued up enough Al Green CDs to last as long as they did. Abbie laughed with pleasure at his careful preparations for her visit. After four years, he was still seducing her like they were on a first date. Peachy took foreplay to mean everything from the evening's sound track to what part of Abbie he wanted to touch first.

"Tell me what you want," he had whispered when they slid into bed, and she knew he meant it, so she did.

Somehow, it didn't seem like the right moment to start talking about vampires in West End, so she decided to wait until morning. But she definitely wanted him to know before Louie Baptiste got there. The problem was she still hadn't thought of a good opening line for what she had to say.

Hey, sweetie, you know the myth of Dracula, right? Well what if I told you . . . Or: *Hey, darlin', guess what's spending some time with Blue and Regina in West End?*

There didn't seem to be a casual way to say it and she knew she had only a few more minutes to rack her brain before Peachy got up and came looking where he knew she could usually be found. The clouds had rolled in thick overnight and it already smelled like rain. She loved the beach in any kind of weather and Peachy did, too. She walked several miles every afternoon, and Peachy went with her as far as his bad knee would let him. They had some of their best conversations walking on that beach. She wished they were walking on it now. Maybe that would make it easier to say what she had to say.

Then she heard Peachy's voice calling her from downstairs. "Up here, darlin'!" she called back.

He arrived with two mugs of hot coffee. "Did I miss it?" he said, handing her an Obama '08 mug and taking the other one for himself, as he settled into the rocker beside her.

"I don't think there's going to be much to see this morning," she said.

"There's always something to see if you know how to look," he said, smiling and pulling his chair over a little closer. "A lady friend of mine taught me that."

Abbie smiled back at him and took a sip of the hot coffee. "She sounds like a very wise woman."

"She is," he said, reaching over to squeeze her hand. "Sexy, too."

The sun broke over the horizon but was immediately enveloped in the low-hanging clouds. The mist was so heavy, she knew that in another minute or two it would probably turn to rain.

"Should we go in?" she said.

He looked at her. "Listen, sweet thing," he said gently, squeezing her hand again, "why don't you tell me what's worrying you so I won't get paranoid and think it's me."

"Oh, no," Abbie said, leaning over to kiss his cheek. "It could never be you!"

"Good, then I can relax. So what is it then?"

Several weak little rays of sunshine were trying to pierce through the clouds but were getting nowhere fast. Abbie decided to just blurt it out, straight no chaser.

"Blue says there are some vampires roaming around West End."

"Vampires?"

Abbie nodded miserably.

Peachy took a deep breath. "You mean like *Dracula*?"

"Sort of like that," she said, "but they don't . . ." She didn't even want to think about it, much less say it. "They don't have to *hurt* anybody. They drink tomato juice."

"Tomato juice instead of . . ." Peachy didn't want to say it, either.

"They're not dangerous, Blue says. At least as far as he knows."

Peachy took a long swallow of his coffee. There was no pre-agreed upon length of time to be taken when absorbing information such as this, so Abbie didn't rush him.

"I think I've adjusted pretty well to you and Blue and the whole past-lives thing," Peachy said, after several long minutes ticked by. "But I gotta tell you, sweet thing, vampires are a whole other kind of thing."

"Tell me about it."

"What do they look like?" he said, sounding more curious than frightened. Peachy had seen a lot, and done a lot. He didn't scare easily. "Do they wear those capes?"

Like most people of his generation, Peachy's idea of a vampire began and ended with Bela Lugosi's brilliant portrayal of the forever-clean Count Dracula slinking through the streets of London, looking for a late-night snack.

Abbie shook her head. "These are all women."

"Vampire *women*?"

"They used to live in New Orleans, but Katrina disrupted their environment so they had to move."

"To West End?"

"No, they're in West End to work with Aretha. They're models."

"Does she know?"

"Not yet. Regina doesn't know it either and she's the one who negotiated the contract."

"What contract?" Peachy was looking more and more confused.

"For the photographs."

He held up his hand. "Okay! Let me see if I got this straight. There are some lady vampires in West End working as models and as long as they drink tomato juice, they don't need to drink . . . anything else."

Abbie was relieved. "That's it exactly, but Blue thinks there's more to it than that."

"Like what?"

"He doesn't know yet. That's why he wants me to talk to Louie."

"What's Louie got to do with it?"

Abbie was famous for the convoluted pathways her stories often took, but Peachy was determined to keep up.

"He knew their family back in Louisiana," she said, the bell announcing his arrival right at that moment as if they had planned it. "I told him to come by this morning and tell me what he knows."

Abbie stood up and so did Peachy.

"Well, I know one thing," he said, following Abbie back into the house. "When I asked you to tell me what was worrying you, vampires hadn't even crossed my mind."

"Welcome to the club."

Chapter Fourteen

Do-Right Men

"They were always a family of women," Louie said after he had reported to Peachy on the day's seafood purchases. Abbie poured him
a cup of coffee and joined them at the kitchen table. "I don't recall
a single Mayflower boy, but they had a gang of pretty girls." Louie
sipped his coffee and nodded approvingly.

"What about their parents?" Abbie said.

Louie frowned a little trying to remember. "No father anybody
knew about, but the mother was tall and light-skinned just like the
girls. Always wore long black dresses. All us kids were convinced she
was some kind of witch."

Abbie and Peachy had talked a lot about witches when they first
got together. One time she had discovered a town in Scotland where
eighty-one people, and their cats, had been executed after a relent-
less witch hunt that went on for months. Three hundred years later,
town leaders had finally apologized, but the statistics had frightened

Abbie who was just learning to embrace her postmenopausal spiritual powers and didn't want to hear anything about people being killed for having visions. Peachy had assured her they'd never have to go anywhere near that town, but he had never forgotten the frightened look on her face.

"Did she claim to be one?"

"Not that I ever heard," he said. "They pretty much kept to themselves most of the time. Every couple of years they'd come to town for a while and then go back."

He was trying to sound casual, but Abbie remembered how startled he had been to hear her speak their family name yesterday.

"Anybody ever go back with them?"

Louie's eyes shifted from Abbie's face to Peachy. "I don't know what you mean."

Peachy shook his head sympathetically. "You might as well tell her what you know, man. She's going to get it out of you anyway."

"The thing is, some of this stuff is just talk, but it might make you nervous."

Abbie sat back in her chair and looked at him. "I'm already nervous."

Louie took his best shot. "What about Blue?"

"Blue doesn't get nervous."

"Okay." Louie sighed and surrendered. "Here's the way it was told to me."

The way he said it made Abbie shiver, and she reached for Peachy's hand.

"The story is that many, many years ago, back when Marie Laveau was still around, there was a family of seven beautiful sisters. The women in this family, as far back as anyone could remember, had been used and abused by the men they chose to marry. The girls' mother herself had been beaten and tormented by the father for years before he finally ran off. Tired of the lying and deception and violence, the mother had decided that she was going to raise her girls with no man in the house. This was fine when they were little, but as they got older, you could see the men who came around counting off the years until they were legal, and you could see those daughters counting, too. Well, their mother didn't want her daughters to suffer the same fate she had when she fell in love with their father." Louie cleared his throat, took a sip of his coffee, and continued. "So one day Madame Mayflower went to see Marie Laveau and asked for a spell to protect her daughters from the charms of unscrupulous men."

"And did she give her one?"

Louie ran his hand over his face and tugged on his chin like he always did when he was nervous or uncomfortable. "Not exactly. Madame Laveau said that if what the woman was looking for was a spell to keep her daughters from having sex with men, even she did not have anything that could guarantee that, but what she could do was make sure the men didn't hang around afterward, which, in her experience, was when the problems usually started."

Abbie understood that. In her experience, men tended to be amazingly agreeable creatures when the promise of possible sex perfumed the air around a woman they were pursuing. The bad times came later.

"Go on."

"So Madame Mayflower said that would be wonderful since she never had been able to see why anybody needed to have a man hanging around all the time anyway. So Madame Laveau mixed her up seven doses of a special potion and told her to wait until the next full moon and then pour it in their left ears while they were sleeping. After that, she promised, Madame Mayflower would never have to worry about her daughters being abused by men." Louie looked at his almost empty cup. "Can I get a refill?"

"Absolutely," Peachy said. He brought the pot over and refilled all three coffees. "So did it work?"

"I guess you could say it did," Louie answered. "Those girls had all the beaus they ever wanted. Whenever they showed up in town, there were always two or three fools who would follow them home."

"But nobody ever bothered them?"

Louie shook his head. "Not that I know of."

"Did they ever marry any of those guys?"

Louie shrugged. "Don't know. None of them ever came back."

Abbie frowned. "Not even for a visit?"

"Not that I recall."

"So didn't anybody ever go looking for them?" Peachy said.

"When a full-grown man follows a beautiful woman off into the woods, whose job is it to tell him he *shouldn't oughta go*?"

Abbie looked at Louie. "There's something else."

"There's nothing else."

"Tell me."

Louie stood up then and walked over to the sliding glass door. Outside, the sun had finally broken through the clouds and the waves were dancing with white caps, but he didn't notice. His voice was so quiet, Abbie could hardly hear him. She leaned forward, straining to catch every word. Peachy did, too.

"Some people said the reason they never came back was because after they were done with a man . . ."—he turned to his friends like this was the last thing he wanted to tell them—"they'd bite off his head."

"Say what?" Peachy stood up so fast his chair fell over.

Abbie closed her eyes and wondered how fast she could get back to Atlanta and tell Blue.

"That was a long time ago," Louie said quickly. "Old lady Mayflower had been dead longer than my grandmother had been alive when she told me that story. Who knows if there's any truth to it?"

Abbie opened her eyes. "Did your grandmother believe it?"

Louie looked at Abbie without blinking. "She said she didn't know whether she did or not, but one thing was for sure."

"What's that?"

"If a man thought a woman could bite his head off if he didn't treat her good, there would be a lot more do-right men in this world."

Chapter Fifteen

A Personal Matter

It was Saturday morning and the West End News was crowded with customers. Every table was full and the line at the counter was almost out the front door. During the week, people tended to come in earlier, pick up what they wanted, and head out to work or school. But on Saturdays, people came in later, hung around longer, and almost always ran into somebody they'd been looking for all week who coaxed them into sitting down for some catch-up. The cappuccino machine was working nonstop behind the counter, and Phoebe Sanderson was making sure every espresso aficionado got that little piece of curled lemon peel in addition to a jolt of pure caffeine via the best Colombian coffee beans this side of Bogotá.

Henry was seated at a small table near the door, greeting regulars and making sure things were running smoothly. One Saturday a month, Blue made himself available to anybody in the neighborhood who needed his attention. It didn't matter if the problem was a dog running around without a leash, or a serious zoning issue that required a call to the right person at city hall, Blue heard every complaint with equal concern and considered every request with equal seriousness.

No appointment was necessary on those Saturdays and the only other person in the room during the exchange was Henry, who never jotted anything down but made sure all of Blue's promises were kept in a fair and timely fashion. In the beginning, there were a lot more requests for protection, but as the neighborhood had become more peaceful, those had pretty much disappeared. People in West End didn't often need to be protected from one another; and when they did, everybody knew whom to call.

In the back room, Blue had just gotten off the phone with Peachy, calling from Tybee.

"We'll leave right after lunch," Peachy said, describing their travel plans. "That will give me a chance to help Louie get set up for tonight and Sunday brunch tomorrow. We'll come on by when we get in."

Peachy and Blue had toured together for so many years, they could communicate in a language of the road, where too much detail could be fatal. They were masters of the coded question. "Anything I need to know right now?"

And the equally coded answer. "It's all good," Peachy said. "Louie had the whole recipe."

"Good," Blue said. "See you tonight."

He had hoped Louie would have some information about these Mayflowers and clearly he did. Not a moment too soon, Blue thought. Regina and Aretha were going to be out with them again all day shooting, and even though he had sent security to their location, there were still some big holes in their story that would be cause for concern until he plugged them.

Henry tapped lightly on the frosted glass, cracked the door open, and stuck his head inside.

"You about ready for another sit-down?"

Blue nodded. "Who've you got out there?"

"There are some guys from Morehouse who would like a word with you," Henry said.

"Students?"

"Graduating seniors."

"They looking for a job?"

Henry shook his head. "Said it was a personal matter."

"I guess nobody told them everything around here is a personal matter." Blue smiled. "How many of them are there?"

"Five." He slid a piece of paper across the table to Blue. "I told them to write down their names and where they're from."

Blue picked up the paper. Each one had written his own name with the same blue pen: Stan Hodges from Trenton, majoring in chemistry; Jerome Smith from Atlanta, a prelaw major; Jackson Stevens from Detroit, majoring in business; Lance Johnson III from Milwaukee, also a prelaw major; and Hayward Jones, a political science major from New Orleans.

"Shall I bring them on back?"

"Sure." Blue folded the paper and put it in his pocket. "Let's see what the next generation's talking about this morning."

Chapter Sixteen

Ordinary Mortals

Aretha was setting up an interesting shot in a history professor's book-crammed office in a big old four-story building with high ceilings, creaky wooden hallways, and one small elevator that squeaked alarmingly above the second floor. Tucked away on a quiet corner of the Morehouse campus, they had somehow eluded the crowds they had generated the day before, and things were going smoothly with a minimum of disruptions.

Once she had set up her lights and positioned the five models in the small space, there was hardly room for Aretha to move around and get the shots she wanted. Regina and Serena didn't even try to squeeze in. An empty classroom across the wide hallway was as close as they could get, which was fine. They were still in the process of evaluating each other, and some time alone was just what they had both wanted.

Serena was busy confirming their deal in principle so contracts could be sent down this afternoon. That was all fine, but Regina still wanted to know why this woman who was so good with details had not mentioned meeting her husband the day before. Of course, she wasn't going to ask her directly. That would come across as suspicious and insecure and she refused to claim either of those emotions. She was hoping for conscious and curious. Conscious of the omission of information. Curious about why.

They settled their business with a promise to exchange the necessary signed documents on Monday and then there was silence. Through the open door of the classroom where they were camping out, they could hear Aretha across the hall, murmuring instructions, offering encouragement and affirmation.

"Good, good . . . keep that. Do more with that. Yes, yes . . . Use that hand more. Good . . ."

"Sounds like phone sex, doesn't it?" Serena said, tucking her BlackBerry into her giant shoulder bag.

"I guess it does at that."

Serena walked over to the big window and looked out at a green expanse of a quadrangle in the middle of the small, beautifully landscaped campus. There was a touch football game in progress, although the players probably should have been in class. Two smiling girls were watching and applauding frequently, so the game was far from over.

"Aretha told me about the big benefit coming up on Saturday," Serena said, introducing a more neutral topic. "She said it's a very big deal around here."

"We do it every year to raise money for one cause or another," Regina said. "My husband and Peachy Nolan started doing it almost twenty years ago. Things were really different around here then. It was like the Wild, Wild West. Once they got it cleaned up, they started raising money to make sure it stayed that way."

"That's admirable." Serena folded her long, lean frame sideways into one of the student desks. "But to tell you the truth, it's still a little too close to the frontier for my taste."

Her comment made Regina feel defensive, but she tried to keep her tone even. "What do you mean?"

Serena rippled her shoulders. "I mean, it's just a matter of time. If your husband hadn't been prepared to take charge, this neighborhood would be just like all the others."

Even though she knew it was true, Regina resented Serena saying it so calmly. "Is that why you dropped in to see him yesterday?"

Serena didn't flinch. "Aretha suggested it. Did she tell you?"

"No," Regina said, hoping she didn't sound like a paranoid, overly possessive wife. "*He* did."

"I see." Serena stretched out her legs in the aisle and crossed them neatly at the ankles. The soles of her black Christian Louboutin pumps were a smooth bright red, as if they had never touched the ground.

"Your husband is a very charismatic man," she said calmly. "I don't believe I've ever seen eyes like that. Do they run in his family?"

There was no hint of discomfort for not mentioning the visit.

"Our daughter has them."

"How wonderful," Serena said. "Those are genes anyone would be proud to pass on."

Regina didn't know what to say to that and before she had time to figure it out, the door opened across the hall and the models strode into the room like they had just been released into the wild.

"I'm starving," said the one whose name was either Sara or Susan, reaching her long arms above her head. Her well-manicured, red-tipped nails brushed the ceiling lightly.

"How can we get something brought in to eat, besides soul food, fake Jamaican jerk, or bad Chinese?" Regina still couldn't tell them all apart, but she thought this was Sasha.

"Are you done?" Serena said, rising from the chair in one long slither and moving past Regina as if she wasn't even there.

"She said we've got an hour for lunch and an hour to change," said the one Regina thought was named Savannah. "So are they going to feed us, or what?"

"The caterer has everything set up for you in the downstairs lobby at the chapel," Regina jumped in. "And the limo is outside to take you across campus."

That seemed to appease them. Even though the walk across the campus was only a couple of hundred yards, she had seen yesterday how difficult it was to get them to walk anywhere in a timely fashion, so for today, Regina had asked Blue if he could give them a driver, just to get them around once they arrived at Morehouse. He had responded with a huge stretch limo that more than accommodated their needs, their legs, and their egos.

"What caterer?" Sheila asked, still sounding suspicious.

"The one I called yesterday," Regina said, as Scylla hovered around them like a mother hen shooing her brood of excitable chicks. "The one who has spent all morning fixing exactly what you like the way you like it."

Sasha tossed her strangely coifed head (they had repeated yesterday's mussed-birdcage style) and rolled her green-lidded eyes. "Well, don't say it like that. It's not like we've been complaining."

At that, Scylla rolled her eyes, too, and let out a strange little hissing noise that didn't sound like anything Regina had heard since she had gone hiking in New Mexico and gotten too close to a big black snake on the trail.

"Scylla!" Serena said sharply, and the sound stopped immediately. "Why don't you get everybody settled in for lunch and I'll be over in a minute to look at the clothes for this afternoon."

"They're hideous," Savannah sniffed. "We're going to look like a bunch of potbellied pigs."

"Then you can eat all the sushi you want at lunch and not have to worry about it," Serena said, as Scylla shooed them out the door.

Regina watched from where she was, still fascinated with their strangeness, but suddenly wary of it, too. What was that sound Scylla had made? She didn't even part her lips, so it was more like a vibration in her chest. Regina wondered if she had ever done it around Aretha.

The models headed down the wide stairway, talking among themselves about whatever they talked about when they were not in the company of ordinary mortals.

When Aretha stepped out into the hallway, Serena fluttered a graceful greeting. "So, how's it going in there?"

"Good," Aretha said, sounding distracted. "They need to be ready again at two."

Serena nodded. "Fine. Should I bring the new contract so we can—"

"I can't talk about that right now," Aretha cut her off quickly, looking at Regina. "Can I see you for just a second?"

"Sure," Regina said, turning to Serena, wondering why Aretha's voice sounded so tense all of a sudden. "We'll talk this afternoon."

"No problem," Serena said, following the others down the stairs. "The sooner the better."

Regina followed Aretha back into the professor's office where they had been shooting and tossed her purse on the desk.

"What's happening?"

Aretha didn't say a word. She closed the door quietly, turned back to Regina, and burst into tears.

Chapter Seventeen

Their End of the Deal

The five young men filed into Blue's office in the same order they had signed the name sheet. Henry came in behind them and closed the door. There were five chairs in front of the table where Blue was sitting, but since no one had indicated that they should take a seat, they remained standing, waiting for instructions.

"Good morning," Blue said pleasantly, standing up and extending his hand. "I'm Blue Hamilton."

"Good morning, Mr. Hamilton," they stumbled over one another to return his greeting. "Good morning."

"Tell me your names," he said, shaking each hand in turn, gauging, as men always do, the strength of the man from the strength of the handshake.

Soft, he thought. *The work they've chosen doesn't require them to use their hands.*

"Sit down, gentlemen," he said, returning to his seat. They sank gratefully into their chairs and he could see how nervous they were. And how young.

He turned to Jerome Smith, sitting on the far right. "You're from Atlanta, Mr. Smith?"

"Yes, sir." Jerome nodded, grateful to be asked a question with an easy answer.

"You from around here?"

"I grew up in southeast, but we knew about West End."

"Good," Blue responded, knowing that meant Jerome had likely told the rest who he was and that making a request for his assistance was not a matter to be taken lightly. This saved everybody a lot of time and confusion as things moved ahead. "So who wants to tell me why you've come to see me this morning?"

Four heads turned to the boy who had taken the middle seat, Jackson Stevens from Detroit.

"Mr. Hamilton, first of all, I want you to know how much we appreciate you taking the time to talk with us."

"That's why I'm here," Blue said.

The boy took a deep breath. "Four years ago, when we were all freshmen, we made a deal, Mr. Hamilton. A bad deal."

"Collectively?"

They looked at one another, then back to Jackson like he was on his own.

"Well," he said slowly, "it was the same deal, but each of us made it individually. And now the people have come to collect. They're only giving us a week and we don't want to go."

"Go where?"

Jackson turned to Stan Hodges, sitting on the far left. "They came to Stan first. Maybe he should start."

Stan swallowed hard. "They contacted me through my Facebook page. I had been complaining about needing some money for school, and they said they had a unique postgraduate program for bright students like me that would pay all of my expenses for four years at Morehouse, starting that same day."

The other four guys were nodding in affirmation like a row of bobblehead dolls.

"That's what they told all of us," Jerome said.

"Do you boys have anything in common besides this deal?"

"No," Stan said. "We're not from the same hometowns. We have different majors."

"Ever play on the same team? Marching band? Anyplace where they might have seen you all together and chosen the five of you specifically?"

"Well, there is one thing," Jackson Andrews said. "We're all real smart."

Blue raised his eyebrows slightly as if none of the evidence pointed him to this conclusion.

"We were all valedictorians of our high school classes," Hayward Jones said. "And we all scored really high on our SATs."

Clearly not an exam that tests for life, Blue thought.

He wondered if they had been duped in some elaborate Internet scheme. Whatever it was, he wished they would just spit it out so he could do what needed to be done and focus his mind on the vamps. Until Peachy got here, it was still all largely conjecture, but he was distracted and these kids were taking too long to get to the point.

"Go on."

"So it sounded like a good deal, you know," Stan said, sounding miserable. "Cost of college these days is ridiculous, Mr. Hamilton. HBCUs cost as much as the Ivy League."

"And in proportion to income, a lot more," Lance Johnson III spoke up for the first time.

Blue wondered briefly if it strengthened a man's resolve to be able to count back three generations every time he signed his name.

"In complex personal matters," Blue interrupted smoothly, "there are always a lot of details that can in some way broaden an outsider's understanding of the issue under discussion. So when I say this, I don't mean to imply that I don't value the specificity of your story."

He looked at each of them as they blinked or coughed or glanced sideways at the man next to them.

"But right now, all I need to know are three things: what was promised, what was delivered, and what was expected in exchange."

Sitting directly behind the guys near the door, Henry nodded slightly as if he could not agree more.

Blue held up one finger. "You've told me what was promised." A second finger. "And was it delivered?"

The five nodded reluctantly, unsure how to tell him exactly what was really going on.

"They paid all your expenses for four years?"

Another collective nod.

"And a stipend," Hayward Jones said, as if in the interest of full disclosure. "So we wouldn't have to get jobs."

"So we could focus on the books," Stan added, as if to justify the money.

"And did you?" Blue said.

They hadn't anticipated the question but they knew the answer did not present them in the best light. Not one of them had held a job during their four years of college and not one of them had maintained an above C average.

"Did we what, sir?" Jerome said, hedging.

"Did you focus on the books?"

The guilty way they evaded Blue's eyes let him know the answer to the question was *Hell, no.* They had enjoyed the free ride but they hadn't upheld their end of the deal. He wondered what piper they would have to pay for their inattention to a small detail like good grades.

Jackson cleared his throat. "We could have done better, Mr. Hamilton. I think I speak for all of us when I admit that we could have done better, but is that any reason to . . ."

His voice trailed off and he glanced at the others, who seemed equally lost for words.

"Good grades? Is that what was expected in return for the support?"

"Not exactly," Stan said, searching for the right word. "We were supposed to *enlist* with them for four years after graduation."

"Like the Peace Corps?"

"Almost like that, Mr. Hamilton," Hayward Jones said, nodding as if he was really relieved that Blue understood. "See, they live on this beautiful, undeveloped island, and we had to promise to live there with them for four years."

"Are there any other men on this island?"

"No, sir. We would be the only ones."

That was when Blue knew what Serena and her tribe were doing in his backyard. These arrogant young fools had signed on as indentured servants to the vamps.

"What did they want you to do on their island?" he said, still trying to get to the heart of the matter. "Manual labor? Clearing the land? Building infrastructure?"

All their heads once again turned to Stan, who took a deep breath and leaned forward, his hands on his knees as much to stop their shaking as anything else. "Look, Mr. Hamilton, I'm going to level with you. We were a bunch of young, dumb guys, okay? They told us all we had to do was"—he cleared his throat nervously—"was to move to their island for a few years and, well, have sex with them twice a day, six days a week."

They watched as Blue's famous eyes darkened as he gazed at them, his face impassive except for a slight ripple in his jaw muscle.

"And when we weren't doing that," Stan continued in a rush, "all we had to do was eat and workout and watch all the sports and porn we wanted."

Blue stood up and walked over to the bar. The boys were desperately hoping for a drink, but he didn't reach for anything. That's why the vamps were here, Blue thought. They had found some genes they thought were worth mixing with their own more rarified DNA and they had come to Atlanta to pick up their order. He turned back to the young men slowly.

"So let me get this straight," he said. "You sold yourselves as stud animals to a group of women you met on the Internet in exchange for a college education?"

They nodded, ashamed, but relieved to get it all on the table.

"We did get to meet them in person, though," Jerome said. "They came down here after we had agreed in principle so we could work out the details and sign the contracts. They rented a house out in Buckhead, one of those big old mansions, and they had us all out to dinner, and, Mr. Hamilton, I don't mean that it was right, but we were only eighteen."

Jackson picked up the story in a whisper. "The things those women did to us that night, Mr. Hamilton. None of us had ever had sex like that before."

"Two of us were still virgins," Stan said. "There was no way really we could have told them no, you know what I mean?"

Blue found it amazing that they thought youthful inexperience could explain such foolish behavior. "Did part of your contract with these women require you to raise any of the babies you'd be making, twice a day, six days a week, for four years?"

"No, sir!" Jerome shook his head quickly. "They told us we didn't have to take any responsibility for the kids."

Blue was saddened by how easily the words rolled off the boy's tongue. Like that was a point in their favor.

"And this didn't strike you boys as strange? That a group of fine women would have to put that much effort and money into finding somebody like you to have sex with?"

Lance III shrugged his shoulders apologetically. "It sounded a little strange, but with all the diseases out there now and how hard it is for women to find a man at all, we just sort of figured they wanted to cut through the bullshit and get the job done. No offense, Mr. Hamilton."

As far as he could see, these guys had willingly signed away four years of their lives as sperm donors. He didn't appreciate Serena not being straight with him, but from where he was sitting, he had no horse in the race.

"So why come to me now when it's time for you to hold up your end of the bargain?"

Stan looked at Jerome, who nodded. "Go on, man. Tell him."

"Mr. Hamilton," Stan said slowly, "are you familiar with the mating rituals of the black widow spider?"

Chapter Eighteen

Shootin' the Breeze

Aretha was beside herself. In the cramped space of the professor's tiny office, she was pacing and crying and threatening to stop taking photographs altogether and go back to being a painter. This was her right, of course, but not such a great idea when a gaggle of sushi-eating supermodels would soon be awaiting instructions for the afternoon and *Essence* magazine was waiting for its next cover shot.

"Tell me what's wrong," Regina said calmly. "Whatever it is, I can fix it."

Aretha stopped in front of Regina and wiped her damp cheeks with an angry swipe of her hand, almost as if she wanted to slap her own face.

"Fix it? You can't fix it, don't you see? I agreed to do something I don't believe in just for the money. I sold out!" She started pacing again. "I don't have the right to call myself an artist. I'm a money-grubbing hack, just like all the others. Sucking up to these *space creatures* so I can buy my daughter all the princess dresses Target can stuff into the Disney aisle. What does that make me, Gina? What the hell does that make me?"

Aretha's meltdown seemed to center on artistic integrity, selling out, and inflicting great harm on Joyce Ann and Sweetie and every other little girl who thought she had to grow tall and stay thin to be considered beautiful.

"How could I even consider such a thing?"

Aretha actually wrung her hands. Regina reached out and stopped the frantic motion.

"Slow down and listen to me." Regina's voice was low and soothing. "Come on now. *Inhale.*"

Aretha did as she was told and drew in a big, shuddering breath. Regina hoped this level of intensity would be reflected in the photographs. If drama was truly part of the process, they should get a museum show out of this one.

"And *exhale.*"

Aretha did, with a *whoosh*. "Okay, I'm listening," she said.

"Are you sure?"

Aretha nodded.

"If you don't want to do it," Regina said slowly, "don't do it."

Aretha blinked like somebody just waking up from a bad dream. "What?"

"Don't do it," Regina said again, releasing Aretha's hands, which had stopped twisting and tugging at each other. "You should never do anything that makes you feel like this."

Aretha offered a shaky smile. "You make it sound so easy."

"There is no *it*," Regina said. "There's just you and me figuring out what you want to do next."

"I worried about this all night! I went home after we took the kids for ice cream and looked at some of the shots from yesterday and they're so beautiful, Gina, but they're just so *wrong*. I don't want any part of foisting this stuff on the public just so I can pay my rent."

"And you don't have to," Regina said. "Finish up what you've got scheduled for today and call it a wrap. I'll tell Ms. Mayflower you're not available to do the portfolio. Period."

"Just like that?"

"Just like that. You haven't even signed a contract yet. Remember, so far we've just been shootin' the breeze."

Aretha fished a tissue that had seen better days out of her pocket and blew her nose loudly. "I guess I'm just not ready for the big time."

"You *are* the big time."

"You don't think they'll get mad, do you?"

"I don't care if they do," Regina said. "I think we can take 'em."

Chapter Nineteen

A Born Buddhist

They decided to leave Abbie's little Civic on the island and ride back together in Peachy's Lincoln. Louie promised to keep an eye on things at the restaurant, but Peachy wasn't worried. The place ran smoothly with or without him there to greet folks at the door, he always said. *It just didn't have as much style.* He was right about that. Peachy had style to burn. With a head full of wavy white hair that was his only real vanity, he looked like what he was: an inveterate hipster who was aging well.

Peachy eased around a big red and white truck with the Target logo emblazoned on the side and glanced over at Abbie. Her eyes were closed, but he knew she was awake. He wasn't worried. By the time they got to Atlanta, he knew Blue would have a plan and he would be there to help implement it. That's the way their partnership always worked and this time would be the same. All he had to do was keep Abbie cool until they got to the city.

"How you doin', sweet thing?" he said gently.

She opened her eyes and turned to him with a less-than-successful attempt at a smile. "I'm okay."

He knew she was a pretty good distance from okay. "So you want to talk about these vampires or what?"

"Do you?"

"Hell, yeah," Peachy said. "What else are we going to talk about?"

"Do you think they're in West End looking for men like Louie said?"

Peachy frowned without taking his eyes off the road. "I thought you said they were here so Aretha could take their picture."

"There are a lot of fashion photographers in New York. Why didn't they use one of them?"

"There's a lot of men in New York, too," Peachy said. "Why would they come all the way here to find something they can round up on 125th Street any day of the week?"

"I don't know," Abbie said.

The small gold hoops in her ears moved against her cheek and she tugged at one absentmindedly. It was all too weird, so they rode in silence. Abbie had taught Peachy to meditate and the two of them were used to sharing silence without feeling any pressure to speak, but today the presence of the vampires was so strong in their minds, they both heard it loud and clear.

Abbie watched a pod of six huge Harleys roar by in the passing lane. She had ridden around Spain on a motorcycle behind her second husband, a painter, back in her early twenties, when she was moving through her expatriate years. She enjoyed the sense of danger riding always gave her, although her husband was a tentative cyclist who never went as fast as she hoped he would.

Sometimes she wished she'd met Peachy when they had had more time in front of them than they had behind, but she didn't dwell on it. If her postmenopausal visions had taught her anything, it was to appreciate the present moment. She loved Peachy *now*. And he loved her the same. Who in their right mind could ask for anything more?

"You know what?" she said.

"What, sweet thing?"

"Let's just try to clear our minds until we see Blue. There's no point in worrying until we know more."

Peachy took her hand and held it gently. "There's no point in worrying *period*."

Her smile was what he'd been waiting for all morning.

"How'd you get to be so smart?"

"Just a born Buddhist, I guess."

Abbie laughed softly at the idea of anything other than some form of Baptist being found in Peachy's tiny hometown. "There are no born Buddhists in Dalton, Georgia."

"Then it must be my lady friend," he said. "The one I was telling you about at sunrise?"

"She's done a good job with you," Abbie said, glad to let the vampires roam around the periphery while she moved Peachy to the center of her Saturday. "And I hear she's not done yet either."

"She better not be," Peachy said. "I ain't half as good as I'm going to be by the time I get through."

Abbie laced her fingers through his, grateful for the strength of his hand.

"I love you, Peachy," she whispered.

"I love you, too, sweet thing," he said. "And you know I got this covered, right?"

"I know."

"Me and Blue been in and out of the rowdiest juke joints in south Georgia and neither one of us ever got cut," he said. "If those vampires start acting a fool, me and Blue got somethin' for 'em."

Abbie wondered what Peachy and Blue would have to use to fight off vampires if it came to that. Was it still necessary to drive a stake through their hearts? The vampires were moving front and center of her mind once again. Peachy must have felt it, too, and he squeezed her hand and turned on the radio.

"We got this," he said again, and she started to respond, until she realized he was talking to himself as much as to her. "Trust me."

Chapter Twenty

Random Humans

It seemed to Blue that everybody in West End needed his attention. Mrs. Robinson was nervous about her new neighbor's pit bull. Mr. Goodwin needed some help with his nephew who was visiting from Chicago and didn't want to obey the house rules. Reverend Dunbar stopped in to say hello, and the owner of the flower shop next door wanted to personally apologize for the owner of the delivery truck who had pulled into Blue's reserved spot yesterday to drop off some birds-of-paradise and raised an objection when he was asked to move.

By the time the last citizen had shaken Blue's hand and been politely ushered out, it was after seven o'clock. Henry made a fresh pot of espresso, poured himself a Diet Coke, no ice, sat down across the table from Blue, and waited with impressive stillness. Henry was not a man who was prone to fidgeting. Their nightly conversation could be wide ranging but tonight there was only one item on the agenda.

Blue downed his espresso and looked at Henry. "Do you think those guys were telling the truth?"

Henry nodded. "At this point, I think they're too scared not to. What do you think?"

"I don't know what those women are," Blue said. "They don't seem to be dangerous to random humans as long as they get their tomato juice, but we need to find out as much as we can about them, just in case."

"Done."

Blue was glad they didn't have to waste any time discussing the possibility of things that could not be rationally explained showing up on your doorstep. Henry had been with Blue long enough to know that not everything could be explained by what you thought you already knew.

"Are you really going to let them take those guys away?"

"I'm prepared to help folks deal with crackheads, sex offenders, thieves, con men, murderers, and unscrupulous land developers," Blue said quietly. "But I think I have to draw the line at vampires. If you don't know better than to make a deal with the *undead,* I can't help you."

Henry nodded again and took a sip of his drink. "I heard that."

"I need to talk to Miss Mayflower."

"Tonight?"

"Tomorrow morning," Blue said. He wanted to get to the bottom of things as quickly as he could, but before he saw Serena Mayflower again, he needed to talk to Regina. "First thing."

"Done."

Chapter Twenty-one

Our Last Hope

When Regina told Serena that Aretha wasn't going to be able to shoot the portfolio after all, she didn't take it well. She didn't raise her voice or threaten legal action or anything like that. She was just a mask of cold fury, demanding a better reason than the honest one. When Regina didn't have one and seemed disinclined to invent one, Serena stalked off with another one of those strange, hissing noises Regina had heard from Scylla. It was such an odd sound. Maybe they were sisters after all and that sound was some kind of weird, genetic tic passing through their family like the wind rustling through dry magnolia leaves.

Relieved that the exchange was over, Regina walked back to her car alone, wondering what Blue would make of the day's events when she shared them over dinner. The last two days had been more than strange and she was glad to close the book on their foray into high fashion. Waving at the campus security officer patrolling the lot on a golf cart, she saw five young men standing near her car wearing identical blue blazers that identified them as Morehouse men.

Fans of the Too Fine Five, Regina figured. *All dressed up to ask for what? An autograph? An email? A chance to simply say hello?* She felt sorry for them, but the closer she got, the less they looked like fans and the more they looked like condemned men considering the menu for their last meal.

"Good afternoon, gentlemen," she said. "I'm afraid the models have already left the campus."

"Oh, we weren't looking for the models, Mrs. Hamilton," one of the boys said quickly. "We were waiting to see . . . to *ask* if we could have a word with you?"

"With me?" she said surprised. "Of course you can. What's on your minds?"

They shifted uncomfortably and looked at the tallest boy, who stepped forward a little.

"Mrs. Hamilton, I'll come straight to the point," he said. "If that's all right with you."

"Please," she said. "I'm all ears."

The boy took a deep breath. "We're asking you to intercede on our behalf and ask your husband to please reconsider our request in light of the seriousness of our situation."

I should have known, Regina thought. People who didn't know how things worked in West End sometimes tried to go around Blue by coming to Regina. It never worked.

"I have no doubt that your situation is serious," Regina said gently. "But I don't involve myself in my husband's affairs."

"We know that, Mrs. Hamilton," another boy spoke up, nervously tugging on the knot of his striped tie. "And under ordinary circumstances we would never, *ever*, ask you to make an exception, it's only that—"

"No exceptions, gentlemen," Regina interrupted him, wondering what had frightened them enough to seek Blue's help by waylaying his wife in a parking lot. "Now if you'll excuse me."

She popped the lock on the driver's side door and turned away from the five miserable faces. Behind her, she heard a desperate voice.

"You're our last hope, Mrs. Hamilton. If your husband doesn't help us, the vampires are going to make us into their sex slaves."

Regina stopped and turned around slowly. *"Say what?"*

The desperate-sounding boy spoke up again. "And when they're done, they'll *eliminate* us."

Regina frowned, confused. "Is this some kind of joke?"

The boys shook their heads in one emphatic motion. "It's real, Mrs. Hamilton. We swear!"

She wondered if they were high on something. They weren't making any sense at all.

"There are no such things as vampires," she said, hoping for their sake it was all a joke. "Somebody's messing with you."

They looked at her and then at one another with obvious disbelief.

"Messing with *us*?" another boy said, his mouth tight and angry. "Like you don't know!"

"Know what?"

"You've been working with them for the last two days!"

"Working with who?"

"Those models are the ones we told Mr. Hamilton about this morning," another anxious boy added his voice to the chorus. "They're the vampires."

He kept talking, but Regina's brain screeched to a halt. *The Too Fine Five? Vampires?*

She made an effort to speak calmly. "You told Blue about this?"

They nodded.

"I need to talk to my husband," she said, sounding much calmer than she felt. "If he wants to get in touch with you, he will."

The boys seemed to realize that was all the reassurance they were going to get from her, in spite of their pleading, so they stepped away, murmuring their thanks for whatever she could do, but when she got in the car and closed the door behind her, the tall one tapped on the window gently.

"Don't let them take us, Mrs. Hamilton," he said, bending to look her in the eye. "I know we did something really, really stupid, but we don't deserve to die for it, do we?"

Regina's mind was whirling, but something in the boy's question brought forth one of her own.

"I don't know," she said. "How stupid was it?"

Chapter Twenty~two

Sharing Their Sushi

Serena had never liked revolving doors. Maybe she came upon them too late in life and just never had time to familiarize herself with them enough to know when to step in and when to step out. The ones you had to push were so narrow that she often found her knees knocking against the glass in front of her and the self-propelled ones were always too slow. She preferred to alight from a limo and have someone in uniform open the door for her. The smiling bellhop in front of the Four Seasons was only too happy to oblige.

"Welcome back, Ms. Mayflower," he said. Serena tipped the guy twenty dollars every time she saw him, which would have earned her such personalized service even without her startling beauty and the notoriety of the Too Fine Five.

She nodded without speaking, swept into the lobby, and headed for the elevators before the gawkers could work up enough nerve to approach her. As she pushed in her security card to gain admittance to the penthouse level, she was thinking about Aretha Hargrove, trying to understand what had made her back out of what Serena had thought was a done deal.

The explanation that Regina had offered apologetically but firmly did not make any sense. Nobody was forcing any little kids to stop scarfing down their Happy Meals. What the hell did negative body images have to do with anything? High fashion wasn't even about the body. It was about the clothes. She had thought any fool would know that, but obviously she had thought wrong.

When Regina asked if she could have a word after they finished the last shot of the day and Scylla had taken the girls back to the hotel, it had never occurred to Serena that she was going to cancel the contract. Not that she cared one way or the other. Aretha had just been insurance to neutralize Blue Hamilton. Now that the portfolio shoot was off, they would stick out like a sore thumb. *Six* sore thumbs.

The elevator doors opened at fourteen. She walked soundlessly down the heavily carpeted hallway and slipped her card in the door of her suite.

"There you are!" Scylla was standing at the wet bar mixing up a big pitcher of Bloody Marys. She had changed into a pair of impossibly skinny jeans and a black cashmere sweater that exposed one smooth shoulder. Her black stilettos were still lying beside the door where she had kicked them off as soon as she walked in. "I was starting to worry."

"I had to clear up a few things with Regina Hamilton." Serena watched Scylla pour two Bloody Marys over ice. "Are we having a party?"

"Sort of," Scylla said, handing one glass to Serena and flopping down on the couch to take a long swallow of the other one. "The stylists are packing up the clothes. The girls are downstairs with plans to gather in Sasha's room later to torture the room service operator, and, as you can see, I have already washed that crap out of my hair and off my face and made us a pitcher of your favorite drink."

Serena dropped her coat on a chair and sank down gracefully on the couch beside her friend. "I am forever in your debt," she said, using a phrase vampires don't take lightly, and taking a big swallow of her own drink. Scylla had tired of the tiny little bottles provided by the minibar, and Serena could see six huge bottles of Campbell's tomato juice and a Texas fifth of Absolut standing at the ready. Scylla had laid in enough supplies for the duration.

"We should toast," she said, looking at Serena.

"What are we toasting?"

"That the first part of this charade is over," Scylla said. "In seven days, we'll be back on our own lovely little island with our own organic, homegrown tomato juice and a fine new batch of absolutely brilliant boys, guaranteeing our immortality for at least another five years."

Serena clinked her glass lightly against Scylla's. "I wish it was that simple."

"It is," Scylla said. "All we have to do now is wait out these next few days, gather up the boys with a minimum of confusion, and get back to where we belong."

Serena sighed. "And where is that, do you think?"

Scylla cocked her head to one side. "What's wrong?"

"Ms. Hargrove has decided she doesn't want to do any more fashion photography."

"You mean after she does our fake portfolio?"

"I mean as of today." Serena kept her voice even. There was no use setting Scylla off any more than was absolutely necessary. "Regina Hamilton said she's concerned about us being a bad influence on little girls because we're so thin."

Scylla just looked at Serena for a minute and then she fell back against the couch cushions and threw her arms up gracefully as if in defeat, while at the same time emitting a deep guttural hiss.

"What's so funny?"

"We're vampires!" Scylla said, wiping the corners of her eyes even though they were incapable of shedding tears of either joy or pain. No longer necessary, the gesture survived only as an evolutionary tick, on its way out like tails and webbed feet. "Being thin is the least of it, don't you think?"

Serena had to agree, glad they had broken the tension of the moment so they could start strategizing.

"This is not really a problem, is it?" Scylla said. "We don't need a reason to be here. We'll go shopping. We'll see the sites. Tourists come here all the time, don't they? *Gone with the Wind* reenactors? King groupies? We'll *blend*."

"That's not going to make Blue Hamilton put out the welcome mat like giving Miss Aretha her big break would have done."

Scylla hissed her displeasure softly. "Please! What's he got to do with anything? All he controls is a tiny little neighborhood in a half-ass southern town."

"You're underestimating him."

Scylla turned back and a small frown made a tiny wrinkle in her very smooth forehead. "So what do you suggest? We can't make her work for us if she doesn't want to."

"Let me think for a minute," Serena said, and closed her eyes.

The reason she was the team leader was testimony to her courage, tenacity, and quick thinking. This was a moment that called for all three. Scylla knew it, too. She moved over to sit closer to Serena, happy to wait as long as it took, settling down so gently, she barely dented the cushion. It didn't take long.

"We'll stay for the benefit," Serena said slowly, the idea not yet fully formed, but good enough to share.

"What benefit?"

Serena tried to remember the details of her brief exchange with Regina before some unscripted conversation about Blue Hamilton's eyes threw everything out of whack. "He hosts a big benefit once a year to raise money for a worthy cause. Everybody who is anybody shows up. We'll buy a couple of tables and promise a great big check."

"What good does that do?"

"He's not going to run us out of town on a rail if we're his biggest contributors. We'll call the press and say we're going to make our first charity appearance."

"You think he'll believe in our sudden philanthropic urges?"

"Of course not. All I'm trying to do is shine a little more light on us so people will want to know where we've gone if we suddenly disappear."

Scylla looked at Serena and narrowed her eyes. "He doesn't have that kind of power."

"He's had more than five lifetimes, remember? Who knows what kind of power he's got?"

"Okay," Scylla said reluctantly. "We'll go to the benefit. When is it?"

"On Saturday, the same night we're taking off with the guys. It would be a perfect place to meet them. Keeps down confusion if they're all in one place."

"They're not going to come voluntarily," Scylla said. "They're already scared shitless."

"That's why they'll be there," Serena said, seeing it more clearly by the second. "So they can be under Hamilton's protection."

"But he can't protect them."

"Exactly."

Scylla hissed softly, recognizing a good plan when she heard one.

"I've got the plane lined up to meet us at the airport Saturday night at eleven thirty," Serena said, sipping her drink delicately. "We'll be gone before midnight."

"Fine." Scylla nodded, but she sounded unconvinced.

Serena stood up gracefully and headed for the door. Scylla didn't move.

"Do me one favor," she said. "The next time you go see Blue Hamilton, take me with you."

Serena turned, her hand on the doorknob. "Don't you trust me alone with him?"

Scylla raised her eyebrows slowly. "No."

Serena's expression didn't change. "I'll keep that in mind."

"Good."

As she pulled the door open, Serena realized that Scylla was still sitting on the couch, watching, but making no move to join her. "Aren't you coming?"

"I don't think so," Scylla said softly. "I've had enough bullshit for one day."

Serena looked at her for a long moment and then stepped out into the hallway, pulling the door closed behind her.

Scylla sat motionless as if listening for the words they hadn't said. Five minutes passed. Then ten. Finally, she stood up, sighed, stretched, grabbed her bag, stepped back into her stilettos, and opened the door. They were too close to the end of this long, strange journey for her to let Serena get distracted by some blue-eyed immortal with a godfather complex.

She picked up her pace, moving toward the elevator quickly with the awkward grace of a long-legged seabird running to take flight. If she hurried, she'd get to Sasha's room before they ordered, which was a good thing. The girls didn't like sharing their sushi.

Chapter Twenty-three

Wolf Bane and a Garlic Necklace

"When were you going to tell me they were vampires?" Regina said, as Blue bent down to kiss her at the front door. Her tone brought him up short, but Blue being Blue, he answered the question as directly as she had asked it.

"When it was time for you to know," he said, as she stepped inside and tossed her purse on the hall table.

She couldn't believe her ears. He was going to play this like a scene from *The Godfather*, but she wasn't feeling like a good Mafia wife at the moment. She was feeling like a righteously indignant African American woman on the edge of a nervous breakdown.

"How can you not tell me I'm doing business with the *undead*?"

Her voice sounded high and tight, but there was nothing she could do about that. On the way home, she had worked herself up with a potent mixture of fear, confusion, and anger. She definitely needed a better answer than that.

Blue closed the front door and stood watching her, but offered no further explanation, which only increased her agitation.

"If Sweetie was here, would you have told me?" she said. "Or would you have let our daughter hang around with them, too?"

"They're not dangerous, Gina."

"How can they not be dangerous?" She heard her voice go up another octave. "Don't they live on—"

Blue cut her off quickly. "Not anymore. Now they drink tomato juice."

"*Tomato juice?*" Regina didn't know whether to laugh or cry. "Are they really vampires?"

He nodded. "Yes, baby, they are."

"Like Dracula?"

"Sort of."

Suddenly she felt dizzy and confused and she swayed on her feet like she was about to faint. Putting his arm around her waist quickly, Blue guided her over to the couch and sat down beside her as she leaned back and closed her eyes.

"Why don't you just bring me some wolf bane and a garlic necklace?" Regina said, opening her eyes.

"You know I would never expose you or Sweetie to any danger," Blue said quietly. "They are not here to do harm to random humans."

The phrase *random humans* did nothing to reassure her. "What do you call making a bunch of college students their sex slaves?"

"That hasn't got anything to do with you," he said. "Those guys made a deal as grown men. Now they have to take responsibility for it as grown men."

Regina's thoughts were swirling around in her head so fast, she couldn't pick just one to bring forward. The whole scene was surreal. She never argued with Blue, and here she was acting like she had just discovered he had a girlfriend stashed somewhere in Buckhead. They had found a way to talk about everything from rehab (her) to reincarnation (him), and all manner of things in between without ever forgetting that they were on the same side. If Blue hadn't told her something this important, he must have a good reason. All she had to do was stop freaking out long enough to let him tell her what it was.

"Okay," she said, "remember when you first told me about how you could remember some of your past lives, not to mention a couple of mine, and it took me a minute to deal with it?"

Blue nodded.

"This is like that. I need you to walk me through exactly what we're talking about."

"Fair enough," he said. "Can I make you some tea while we talk?"

She nodded. His arm stayed around her waist as they walked to the kitchen.

"I'm sorry that however you have heard this, it was not the way you would have heard it from me."

"Then let's pretend I haven't heard a thing," she said. "Let's just let this be an ordinary Saturday at the Hamilton house. Begin at the beginning. . . ."

Chapter Twenty~four

Stupider and Stupider

"What kind of shit have you got me in now?" Peachy said when Blue opened the door to him and Abbie an hour later. Peachy was carrying a huge cooler and trying to sound casual. "Baptiste sent his respects and enough food to feed the neighborhood. I'll put it in the back."

Blue reached out to take Abbie's hand and drew her in for a hug. He could feel the tension in her body as she leaned into his embrace.

"How you doin'?" he said, closing the door behind her, but keeping one arm lightly around her shoulders.

"I'm okay. Where is everybody?"

"Sweetie's on a sleepover and Gina's upstairs changing."

"What did she say when you told her?"

"I didn't. She ran into some Morehouse guys on campus and they told her before I had a chance."

"Oh, no!" Abbie said, imagining how shocked her niece must have been to hear such a thing from strangers. "How did she take it?"

"Pretty well," Blue said, walking her into the living room.

Abbie didn't believe that for a second. She sat down on the couch while he took his usual seat in the big chair near the fireplace where he used to sit and smoke a nightly cigar, but which had now become his daughter's favorite place to curl up in his lap for a bedtime story. Abbie looked tired, but she tried to smile so he wouldn't see how worried she was.

"So what's the plan?" Peachy said, coming in from the kitchen with a bottle of red wine and a corkscrew in one hand and four glasses in the other. He handed the wine to Blue, put the glasses on the coffee table, and took a seat on the couch.

"I'm working on it," Blue said, opening the wine and pouring three glasses. "What did Baptiste say?"

Abbie accepted the glass Peachy offered her and tucked her feet up under her purple crinkle skirt. Peachy looked over at her and patted the cushion next to him.

"Come closer, sweet thing," he said gently. "This ain't no time to keep your distance."

Abbie moved a few inches closer, and Peachy made up the difference with a graceful slide in her direction, careful not to spill the wine.

"Shouldn't I wait for Gina?"

Blue shook his head. "No, go ahead. We'll catch her up when she comes down."

Abbie took a deep breath. "Louie said years ago there was a family of women who had suffered at the hands of men for generations, so their mother got a potient from Marie Laveau, trying to protect them."

"The voodoo queen?"

Abbie nodded. "Except the potion made them use men sexually, and then . . . and then . . ." She hesitated, searching for the right way to say it.

"They bite their heads off?" Blue said.

"You knew?" Peachy took a big swallow of his wine.

"Five guys from Morehouse came by the West End News. Said they'd signed a contract."

"A contract where you agree to let somebody take your head off at the end?" Peachy sounded incredulous.

"That's right."

"No, that's *crazy,*" Peachy said. "What did they get for their trouble?"

"Full scholarships and four years of unlimited porn, ESPN, and vampire sex."

"That's all?"

Blue nodded. "That's it."

Peachy shook his head. "That is some stupid shit, you know that?"

"How did they ever get them to agree to such a thing?" Abbie said.

"They didn't read the fine print," Blue said, leaning to refill Peachy's glass.

"Stupider and stupider," Peachy muttered.

"What do they want you to do?"

"Protect them from the vamps."

"What did you tell them?"

Blue looked at Abbie and chose his words carefully. "I told them I would consider their request, but as far as I could see, I had no role in the dispute."

"But you can't just let them go!" Abbie said, shocked that he would even consider washing his hands of the whole thing.

Before he could answer, Gina walked into the room and looked at Abbie like she was a stranger. "I can't believe you knew about this and didn't tell me."

"Blue told me just before I left for the island," Abbie said. "He . . . we were sort of hoping that they would clear out before we had to tell you anything about their proclivities."

"So if I hadn't heard it on the street, you were just going to let me keep doing business with a bunch of vampires?

"We should have told you before," Blue said. "I'm sorry."

She looked at Abbie and then back to Blue, still too confused to be scared and too scared to be angry. There were so many questions she wanted to ask as soon as she was sure she could handle the answers.

"Hey, Peachy," she said, as if seeing him for the first time.

"Hey, darlin'," he said, pouring her a glass of wine. "You look like you could use this."

She took the wine and walked over to the window. Outside, Aretha's bright red truck pulled up in the front of the house. "Have you told Aretha yet?"

Blue shook his head. "Not yet."

"Well," she said, going to answer the bell, "now's your chance."

Chapter Twenty-five

Speak of the Devil

Aretha took it better than they thought she would. Once she understood that the tomato juice really worked, she stopped being scared and started being mad. She was mad at Blue for not telling them the minute the boys came to see him. Then she was made at Mayflower and company for having the nerve to think they could come waltzing into West End, pluck out five young black men, and leave without expecting consequences.

They settled in at the kitchen table because Regina said that nothing could be really scary in the room where they had all shared so much love and laughter, and because Peachy had the restaurateur's faith in the soothing power of good food. Two hours later, they were still sitting there over coffee, but no closer to any real understanding.

"They're checking out of their hotel on Saturday," Blue said, passing on the information Henry had gathered. "So I guess they intend to wrap up their business here by next week."

"Their business is done now as far as I'm concerned," Aretha said. "Let's call the police."

All three heads turned in her direction. They didn't know exactly what was going to happen next, but Blue Hamilton wasn't about to call the Atlanta Police Department and ask for their assistance running some vampires out of West End.

"Call them and say what, darlin'?" Peachy spoke for the group. "This ain't exactly what they taught 'em at the police academy."

"We've got to do something," Regina said, putting down her cup. "Those kids were worried sick. You should have seen them. They were literally shaking in their shoes."

"I wouldn't be surprised," Blue said, and the coldness in his voice surprised her. "They didn't strike me as particularly courageous."

"Later for them," Aretha said. "It's their fault we're even dealing with this madness. How do you think I feel? Taking pictures of vampires all day? That's why they didn't want to get too close to Dr. King's statue. That much evil can't stand to be too close to anybody that good. I should have known right then! *Jesus!*"

"Calm down," Abbie said gently. "No reason to get all excited until we get a better handle on things."

"Too late," Aretha snapped. "I'm way past all excited and moving right into semihysterical."

They sat in silence for a moment, the last of their coffee cooling in their cups.

"What are you going to do?" Regina finally said.

"I've already taken care of security for you and Aretha until they leave," Blue said. "And I've got somebody at their hotel twenty-four hours. Don't worry."

"Yeah, right," Aretha said. "How exactly are we supposed to do that?"

"I mean, what are you going to do about the boys?" Regina said.

Blue's voice was a low rumble. "Did they tell you what they wanted me to do specifically?"

"They want you to stop the vampires, of course."

"But did they tell you how I'm supposed to do that?"

"If they knew that, I don't think they would have been following me all over the parking lot."

"How do you stop a vampire anyway?" Peachy said. "If you had to do it for some reason."

Aretha stood up suddenly and started clearing dishes off the table. "Well, in the movies, they just pry open their earth-filled coffins and drive a stake through their hearts. How about that?"

She dropped the dishes in the sink with a clatter, but before anyone could protest or propose a less-violent alternative, Regina's cellphone chirped on the counter. The recently added ringtone was the theme song from *The Addams Family*.

"Speak of the devil," Aretha said, checking to make sure she hadn't actually broken anything but noticing a couple of saucers had been chipped.

Regina looked at Blue. Without a strategy, how much information was she supposed to give away? Her last exchange with Serena had been to tell her that the portfolio was off, and they had not parted well.

"Answer it," Blue said. "And don't tell her anything you didn't know last time you two had a conversation. Okay?"

She nodded and cleared her throat. "Ms. Mayflower? What can I do for you?"

As she listened, the others tried unsuccessfully to imagine the other half of the conversation. Returning to her seat, Aretha laid her hand lightly on Blue's shoulder in passing by way of apology, but there was no need. No reaction to the news they had shared today could be called extreme, and what were a few chipped saucers among friends for life?

"Yes, this coming Saturday night," Regina said.

Peachy raised his eyebrows. There was nothing going on around here this Saturday night but the benefit and they all knew it.

"Yes, there are a few tables left," Regina said. "They seat six."

Aretha leaned even closer to the phone, but Serena's speaking voice was a soft hum even face-to-face. It was impossible to eavesdrop.

"Well, yes, of course, certainly. Yes, it is a very worthy cause and I'm sure they'll know how to put your contribution to good use. Thank you. Yes, I will. Thank you."

Regina just sat there for a minute like she hadn't quite absorbed the conversation, and then she looked at Blue and shook her head slowly.

"What, baby?"

"She said there's no hard feelings about Aretha changing her mind, and since they're going to be here for another week doing a couple of music gigs, they wondered if there were any tables left for the benefit."

"*Our benefit?*" Peachy sounded incredulous and indignant.

"Because they'd like to buy a table for six *and* make a donation of"—she paused, still not believing she had heard Serena correctly—"fifty thousand dollars."

Abbie gasped. "Fifty thousand dollars?" She wondered if the group of nonviolent men who were this year's benefit recipients would be willing to accept such largesse from a bunch of decidedly violent vampires.

"What did you tell her?" Aretha said.

Regina looked at Blue. "I told her I'd see her Saturday."

Chapter Twenty~six

An Escape Clause

Sunday

The next morning, when Serena arrived at the West End News, Blue was already at his table reading the Sunday *New York Times*. Henry brought her through the private entrance and Blue rose to greet her, but this time he didn't offer coffee. They sat down across from each other with the cautious wariness of two seasoned prize fighters entering the ring.

"Do you know why I asked you to come here this morning?" Blue said.

"I assumed you wanted me to pay for our table in advance," Serena said, crossing her long legs with a swish of black silk stockings.

Blue's eyes never left her face.

"I am very disappointed that you didn't see fit to tell me about your arrangement with the Morehouse students."

Her expression didn't change, but her eyes took on the wariness of a predator, unexpectedly encountering one of its own.

"As I understand it, the college is not technically under your . . . jurisdiction."

Blue had no interest in discussing boundaries and borders with someone who was unable to appreciate the value of either one. "Do you really think I'm going to allow you to come here and take five free black men away as stud animals?"

"No one twisted their arms, Mr. Hamilton," she said calmly. "Yes, they signed over four years of their young lives, but that's not so different from enlisting in the navy or signing a contract for the run of a Broadway show, is it?"

"You didn't tell them you were going to bite their heads off when you were done."

She looked at him and shook her head in slow motion, as though reprimanding him. "They declined the information."

"What do you mean?"

"After we described the sex and the scholarships and the free porn and the nonstop sports, we told them there was one last piece of information that was so secret, it could be revealed to them only if they wanted to see it badly enough that they would agree to give up something."

"What?"

"The free porn."

Blue looked at Serena and he knew. Given a choice between potentially lifesaving information and four years of unlimited porn? They probably didn't hesitate more than ten seconds. If that.

"Exactly," Serena said, reading his silence correctly.

Blue felt the weight of these young men's choices and he didn't like it one bit. Their stupidity had put him in a position of bargaining for their survival with a vampire who was holding all the cards.

"They are certainly young fools, but last time I checked, that was not a capital crime," he said, thinking how cold her face remained, no matter the topic of conversation.

Serena sighed as if the whole subject was exhausting. "There are two schools of thought about this, Mr. Hamilton. One group wants to hold on to our most ancient and sacred rituals."

"Like the biting off of a man's head?"

"That is our tradition, Mr. Hamilton. We were born to it, but like any group that wants to survive, we have to adapt. Some of us recognize that fact and, as an alternative, we advocate the development of a race of men worthy of living among us as peers, as lovers, as fathers, as friends. Men we can trust with our hearts and our minds and our lives and our bodies and our children."

She looked at Blue without blinking. "But we have no experience with men like that, Mr. Hamilton, so it's hard to argue for a more significant male presence on our small island."

"People are not allowed to sell themselves for breeding and slaughter," Blue said.

"I told you this was a moment of transition for our little tribe," Serena said. "But until that transition is complete, we need those boys, as weak and sorry as they are, to ensure our survival. Unless of course . . ."

She held the silence long enough for Blue to prompt her. "Unless what?"

"Unless you're prepared to go in their place," she said, watching his face for a reaction.

"I'm not in the business of making babies that I'm not going to stay around to raise."

"You could raise them if you wanted to," Serena said softly. "We're certainly not going to kick *you* off the island."

Blue kept his face impassive, but his eyes were as intense as hers.

"You might find out we're not half as bad as they say."

"You're a thousand times worse."

Serena raised her eyebrows. "I'm surprised to hear you say that, Mr. Hamilton," she said. "After all, you're not that different from us when you think about it."

"All of my lives come to an end."

"What if this one didn't have to?"

"You don't have that kind of power."

"But if I did?"

"You don't."

Serena sighed again. "They signed a contract, Mr. Hamilton." She dug around in her bag and took out a white business envelope, which she extended to him. "You can take this copy for your perusal."

Blue accepted the envelope and slipped it, unopened, into his inside coat pocket.

Serena smoothed her hair. "Look, Mr. Hamilton, there is no reason for this to be a problem to either one of us."

"I don't expect it to be," Blue said.

"Did they tell you that there is an escape clause?"

"An escape clause?"

She nodded. "It is possible, even at this late date, for them to void the contract. They've got until next Saturday night to bring witnesses forward to testify on their behalf."

"Witnesses?"

"I'm surprised they didn't mention it," Serena said. "All they have to do is get one woman to speak up for them in front of a group of ten or more people."

"Speak up for them how?"

"Give testimony as to their worth and value," she said. "Be a witness for how much they are loved and needed by all who move within their sphere."

"Any woman?"

"A woman of their choosing. The names are already on the contract."

"That's it?"

Serena nodded. "You'd be amazed, Mr. Hamilton, at how few men have any women they can call upon to speak up for them, no matter how grave the consequences of remaining silent." She reached into her bag again and took out a huge pair of sunglasses.

"There are probably any number of women prepared to speak up for you, including your wife, who by all accounts loves you deeply and would probably find it inconceivable to trade you away for any amount of treasure. But you are the exception, Mr. Hamilton, not the rule."

"Are you saying you don't think any of these women will speak up?"

Serena shrugged with her trademark ripple. "I don't know. Feel free to ask them. They all live in Atlanta."

"Did you tell them these young men would not be back?"

He could see her choosing her words carefully.

"When we talk to them, we liken our little experiment to working on a space station," she said. "We tell them there are great risks, which is why we offer them such generous compensation for their cooperation."

"How generous?" Blue said, suddenly realizing that securing these testimonies might not be as easy as he had thought it would be.

"A quarter of a million dollars," Serena said, slipping on her enormous sunglasses and standing up to go. *"To each and every woman on their list."*

Chapter Twenty-seven

A Beating Heart

When Aretha rang the bell early that Sunday morning, Regina was already searching the Internet for other ways to kill a vampire that didn't involve her husband wearing a big black cape and pounding sharpened tree trunks into the skinny chests of the Too Fine Five. She knew that Blue had been involved in many kinds of violence in his line of work, but never against women or anything that looked like women. She had hardly slept a wink during the night because her dreams were full of Blue and Peachy and the others, roaming West End with old-fashioned lanterns, looking for the vamps. And then when they found them, how exactly did that stake thing work? Did they give them chloroform or something first so they wouldn't struggle? Did chloroform even work on vampires? Did they feel pain? She seemed to remember a few bloodcurdling screams at the end of the old *Dracula* movie as Dr. Van Helsing, the vampire-killing scientist, finally caught up with the Count and his wives in that coffin-filled basement, but she couldn't be sure.

Not that the details really mattered. Screaming or not, she didn't want Blue to have to do it. *Period.* There was a limit to what people could ask of her husband, or there should be, she thought, scrolling past a picture of a vampire in a long white gown, sinking her bloody fangs into the neck of some poor, unsuspecting man who seemed oblivious to her wraithlike presence hovering above his chest. Sometimes she thought about Nina Simone singing in that live recording "You give up everything you got, trying to give everybody what they want."

That was Blue all right. He never said no, even when the task was crazy, like this one. *But not me,* Regina thought. She didn't intend to let him use up his *everything,* fighting off a bunch of vampires with a sharpened stick. There had to be another way, and she intended to find it before Saturday night, but she had been on the computer since Blue left at seven, and so far nothing new. It seems people had tried other things over the years, including guns, knives, swords, hot oil, heavy stones, and fire, but nothing really worked, so they always came back to the old tried and true.

She was so deep into reports of a recent vampire scare in Malawi, which actually brought down a government thought to be infested, that she jumped when the bell rang, as if somebody had yelled "Boo" in her ear. Aretha was standing on the porch, looking miserable when Regina opened the door.

"I'm sorry to bother you . . . ," she began, but Regina didn't even let her finish. She reached out and drew her inside.

"I was going to call you," she said, hugging her friend hello, "but I knew you were working."

"Not anymore," Aretha said, slipping off her jacket and unwrapping a long orange scarf from around her neck.

"What are you talking about? The portfolio is off, but they still have to pay you for the . . ." Regina stopped in midsentence, realizing what she was saying.

"Exactly," Aretha said. "I can't take money from *Essence* for those pictures. It was bad enough when I just thought those girls were weird, but now that I know *how* weird? No way!"

"Come on," Regina said. "I'll make us some tea."

Aretha followed her into the kitchen and watched her put on the teakettle.

"I went home last night after we all talked and looked at some of the pictures, and I won't lie. It's very interesting work," she said, pacing in front of the sink. "All that stuff we did in the office after I decided I wasn't doing the portfolio is very strong. I was really able to use that anger."

Regina got down two mugs and a Celestial Seasonings sampler.

"But I'm not using my art in the service of those vamps. It's not right." She leaned over and selected a chamomile for herself and a Morning Thunder for Regina, who was addicted to it. "Even if the pay is fabulous!"

The kettle gave a little prewhistle moan and Regina turned it off quickly and filled their cups with the steaming hot water.

Aretha dunked the teabag ferociously up and down. "I hate this."

"Me, too," Regina said.

"So does this mean that Blue and Peachy are going to have to—"

"We don't know anything specific yet," Regina interrupted her quickly. "Blue will see Serena this morning to see if he can talk her out of it."

"And if he can't?"

Since she had no good answer, Regina was relieved that the doorbell gave her an excuse to leave the question hanging in the air.

"Relax," she said, getting up and patting Aretha's shoulder lightly. "That's my Sweetie coming home. She spent the night with Abbie."

At the front door, Abbie stood alone, holding Sweetie's Dora the Explorer backpack. She greeted Regina with a hug. "Your daughter is doing errands with Peachy. They'll be along later."

"Aretha's in the kitchen," Regina said. "Come on in and have a cup of tea with us. I've been on the Internet all morning, but so far, nothing we can use."

"I've been looking, too," Abbie said. "The only thing that seems to be foolproof is—"

"That's not an option," Regina said, cutting her off. "We have to keep looking."

Abbie nodded and handed Regina the backpack. "Gina?"

"Yes?"

"Are we okay?"

Regina looked at Abbie. "We're fine, but promise me one thing?"

"Anything."

"No more secrets? About anything?"

"It's a deal!" Abbie said, hugging Regina again, relieved. "Now, where's my favorite photographer?"

Aretha stopped pacing long enough to hug Abbie, who looked at her and frowned. Regina recognized that look. It was the one Abbie always gave her when she was feeling off-center and responsible for things that were clearly beyond her control.

"How you doin', darlin'?"

"I've been better," Aretha said.

"Don't blame yourself for this," Abbie said, sitting down and pulling Aretha gently into a chair. "They were jut using you as an excuse to hang around. It doesn't have anything to do with you."

Aretha's eyes filled with tears. "That's what I keep telling myself, but I still feel like it's my fault."

"Well, don't," Abbie said firmly. "It isn't."

"It will be if I don't call *Essence* and tell them under no circumstances should they use those photographs," Aretha said, getting up to pace again. "It will be if—"

"Don't call anyone," Regina said, surprised at the sharpness in her own voice. Aretha froze. "Don't tell anyone. Don't do anything."

No one said anything for a minute, and then Aretha sat down again next to Abbie.

"Don't you get it?" Regina said softly. "Abbie and I have been up all night trying to find some way to get these vamps out of here without Blue and Peachy having to do something that will change them forever."

"What do you mean?" Aretha whispered.

Abbie reached over to take her hand.

Regina said the words she'd been trying not to say all morning.

"I mean, you can't drive a stake through a beating heart and emerge unscathed."

Chapter Twenty~eight

A Little Bad Judgment

Monday

When the big black Lincoln pulled up beside each boy and the driver stepped out to motion them over, their reactions were identical: They looked around for somewhere to run. But before they could will their feet to risk it, they remembered that black town cars were Blue Hamilton's vehicle of choice. Panic gave way to desperate hope as they recalled their brief exchange with Mrs. Hamilton the day before. Maybe she had put in a good word with her husband after all. Maybe he wanted to tell them how he planned to save them. One by one, they piled into the car for what Jake promised would be a brief meeting with Mr. Hamilton at the West End News. They wished they could ask one another what was up, but they were too intimidated to do anything but make eye contact and hope for the best.

Henry met them at the rear door and ushered them immediately into the back room where Blue stood waiting for them. They filed in with their heads bowed and stood in a line in front of Blue as if they had been called to the principal's office. Henry's massive, silent presence behind them blocked their only possible escape. Blue didn't say anything for a good thirty seconds. He just looked from one young man to the next, and even though none of them had the nerve to lift their eyes, they could feel his stare like it was burning a hole in their scalps.

"Look at me," Blue said finally, his voice harsh. They raised their heads slowly, each boy hoping his eyes would not be the first pair he would meet. As it turned out, that distinction went to Stan Hodges. Blue gazed at him so long, Stan actually thought he might pass out. He had never seen eyes that cold. Even on the vampires, there was a spark of *something* moving. But there was no light in Blue Hamilton's eyes.

"I understand that when you came to see me for help a few days ago, you neglected to mention a very important element of your dilemma."

The boys could feel one another's discomfort, but they kept their eyes locked on Blue. Nobody said a word. They realized he probably didn't expect them to.

"But this morning it came to my attention that you already have a possible solution to your problem. Anybody want to tell me what that is?"

Four heads turned to their unofficial spokesman. Stan Hodges took a deep breath to calm himself as best he could before trying to explain the situation in a way that didn't make them look like complete fools.

"We have an escape clause."

"And what are the terms of that clause?"

Stan swallowed and looked at Jerome for backup.

"Well, Mr. Hamilton, *sir*, it was kind of like a character-witness thing."

"Be specific."

"If we can produce one woman who would come forward and speak on our behalf, we don't have to go."

"I see," Blue said. "Then what is the problem?"

Jerome's nerves failed him and he looked over at Jackson.

"There have been some issues," Jackson said. "Some communication problems, you might say."

Blue frowned. "What does that mean?"

"You know how it is with women," Lance said, and was immediately sorry when he saw Blue's expression. "I mean *sometimes*, how it is with *some* women. You can't please them no matter what you do."

Stan tried to steer the conversation back around to the matter at hand. "The thing is, Mr. Hamilton, all these particular women have to do is vouch for us one time and we're free to go, but they refuse. And no matter what we say, they won't budge. We need somebody to talk to these women, to help make them come to their senses. That's really why we came to you, but we didn't know exactly how to explain it."

"I see," Blue said again and looked at each of them in turn. "You want me to convince some women I've never met to absolve you of whatever crimes made them cut you loose in the first place, not because you're sorry and you want to make it right, but because you're trying to get out of a deal you made of your own free will?"

There was a long moment of silence. They searched their brains for a more positive spin, a more generous interpretation of the question, but the silence lengthened and grew, and still nobody said a word.

Finally, Lance leaned forward and tried a small, ingratiating smile. "I mean, look, Mr. Hamilton, nobody's perfect, right? We're young. Nobody taught us how to treat women, so we're going to make some mistakes until we figure it out, right?"

From where Henry stood, he thought Blue looked more sad than angry. The boys squirmed uncomfortably under his gaze.

Stan couldn't stand it any longer. "Mr. Hamilton, we're begging you. Please help us."

"I won't give aid or assistance to your enemies," Blue said. "But I can't stand with you. I think your witnesses have the right to their own opinions."

Henry opened the door behind them and they realized to their dismay that the conversation was over. Jerome and Hayward looked like they were about to cry. Lance's expression was a twisted mask of disbelief. Stan caught a glimpse of Jackson's terrified face beside him and appealed to Blue one last time.

"I know you don't have to help us, Mr. Hamilton." His voice was flat and miserable. "I don't pretend to understand why you won't, but before you write us off, I beg you to ask yourself one question. What kind of women would send a man off to such a terrible fate just because he exercised a little bad judgment?"

Blue's eyes were hard and his voice was cold. "Any time your life is at stake and you can't find even one woman to come forward and say, 'This is a good man,' your problem isn't what kind of women *they* are. Your problem is what kind of men *you* are."

Chapter Twenty~nine

What You Get Used To

Regina was glad Peachy had brought so much food. When she and
Blue found themselves alone in the kitchen at the end of the long,
strange day, it was good to have the makings of a great meal already
at hand. She told Blue that Aretha was still pretty freaked out, but
that she had agreed to not to call the people at *Essence* and read
them the riot act for hiring her to photograph some vampires, in the
interest of keeping down a general panic when it would dawn on the
magazine people that she wasn't kidding.

At Regina's suggestion, she had sent Joyce Ann to spend a few
days at her father's house in midtown until things settled down without mentioning the real reason she wanted her daughter out of West
End. Aretha trusted Blue with her life, but this was different and
they all knew it. Sweetie was spending the night with Abbie, and
one of Blue's most trusted associates would be parked right outside

until she was safely home in the morning. Regina needed to talk to Blue alone.

"So that's all I've got," she said, wanting to know more about Blue's meeting with Serena than he'd been willing to tell her on the phone. "Your turn."

Blue leaned over to where he had hung his jacket on the back of a kitchen chair and took out the contract Serena had given him earlier.

"There's an escape clause," Blue said. "If any of the guys can find a woman who will speak up on his behalf, the contract is null and void and everybody's free as a bird."

Regina felt relieved. "Then what's the problem? I'll speak up for them if that's all they need."

Blue shook his head and handed her the bulky white envelope. "It has to be somebody who knows them a little better than you do. Somebody they designated when they first signed up."

Regina flipped through the pages of the contract quickly, her eyes scanning for the words *escape clause*. "What do you mean? Like a testimony to their good character?"

"Something like that," Blue said. "They've got specific language for what she has to say."

"Here it is," she said, reading aloud. "The woman listed below will stand before a company of not less than ten people and both signatories and swear and affirm the following. This man is a good man who can be trusted to tell the truth, live peacefully among others, assist in the care and raising of his children, and contribute to the overall stability and productivity of his community."

Regina frowned. "So why don't they call up these designees and send the vampire girls packing?"

"Because none of the women they listed will come forward."

"You don't mean these women are prepared to just let these guys go?"

"That seems to be the situation."

Regina couldn't believe Blue was serious. "Does it say anything about who they are to these guys?"

"Look on the last page," Blue said.

Regina turned to it. "High school sweetheart, best friend, neighbor, babymama, grandmother." She looked up. "Grandmother?"

Blue nodded. "That's what it says."

"Do they know their silence will be consigning these boys to death?"

"I don't think they care."

"That's not possible." Regina stood up and walked over to the back window. Outside, the moon was lighting up the freshly turned garden, and she felt like the ground where she was standing had shifted underneath her feet. Had it finally come to this? Had all the bad times and betrayals finally broken the bonds she thought were unbreakable? She turned back to her husband, who was watching her intently.

"Black women have defended black men against everything from the slave master to the crack pipe ever since our feet hit American soil," she said. "It's who we are! There is no way five black women are going to surrender our best and brightest to some vampires without a fight!"

"Apparently in this case that code isn't being observed," Blue said. "The reason the boys came to me was to ask for my help in convincing those women to change their minds."

"Then that's what you have to do," Regina said. "There's not a woman in West End who would refuse to step up once you make them understand what's at stake."

"I can't do that, Gina."

She turned back to Blue. "Why not?"

"I'm not prepared to second-guess a woman who tells me she's lost respect for a man," he said. "I have to respect her truth. Isn't that what you always tell me?"

"Black women don't have the luxury of walking away from our men."

"Even when they fall short of the mark?"

"*Especially* when they fall short of the mark."

He raised her palm and kissed it softly, his mustache tickling just enough to make her wish somebody would call and say it was all a mistake, but she knew that was just a dream. This was real life, and she was going to have to figure out a way to deal with it, *vamps and all.*

"That's not much of a deal, is it?" Blue said softly.

"You know what my grandmother used to say?"

"What, baby?"

"It's not what you like. It's what you get used to."

"So what are you going to do?" Blue said.

Regina didn't blink. "I'm going to go see those women myself and see if I can get them to agree to give these boys one more chance to get it right."

"What if they don't deserve another chance?"

"Everybody deserves another chance." Regina sighed.

Something in her weariness moved her husband. It was the same weariness he had seen in his mother's face when she tried to find something to love in between his father's angry rampages. It was the smallest glimmer of a desperate hope that something would change for the better, even when it never did. *Everybody deserves another chance.* Who was he to deny her that?

"How about if we invite them over to West End and you can talk to them together?" he asked. "That might make it easier."

"It would," she said. "But that's okay. I know you don't care about these guys."

He looked at her. "I care about *you.*"

"Thank you, baby," she said. "Don't let me forget it, okay?"

"I promise."

"I'm exhausted," Regina said, and she kissed his cheek lightly. "I'm going to turn in."

"All right," he said. "I'll be up directly."

But halfway up the stairs, he called her name.

"I know you think this is how to love us, baby," he said softly when she turned back toward him. "But no woman can love a weak man hard enough to make him strong."

She smiled at him in the dim light. "No law against trying, is there?"

Chapter Thirty

By Blood or by Love

Tuesday

The next day, Regina called each woman and identified herself as Blue Hamilton's wife. In no instance did anyone answer *Who?* There was usually a brief pause and then a fairly tentative *Yes?* Reassuring them immediately that everything was fine, Regina invited each one to come by the West End News and speak with her and her husband about the contract they had signed with one Ms. Serena Mayflower a few years back. This was followed by another long pause.

"We'll send a car for you tomorrow around five thirty," Regina said, as they searched their brains for a way to decline the invitation. "And I promise not to keep you more than an hour."

"We didn't do anything wrong," Jerome Smith's grandmother, Alice, had said, sounding nervous.

"Nobody's accusing you," Regina replied soothingly. "We've just got some information that my husband wants to share before you make any final decisions."

"What kind of information?" Hayward Jones's high school sweetheart, Jennifer Monroe, had wanted to know.

"The driver will be there at three," Regina said. "I look forward to seeing you then."

Blue had agreed to host the gathering and do most of the talking. Regina thought that would give them the best chance of succeeding with at least one of the potential witnesses.

At Regina's suggestion, Blue had high tea prepared for his visitors. One table held an elaborate silver tea service, delicate bone china cups, and a mouthwatering assortment of pastries and fresh fruit. When the women were ushered through the entrance to Blue's private office at the rear of the West End News, Regina welcomed them as if it were her home. She told them her husband would be there momentarily and offered refreshments while she tried to put their names with their faces.

Judy Hughes, a friend of Stan Hodges; Kendra Brownlee, Lance Johnson III's self-described babymama; Louise Solomon, Jackson Stevens's neighbor; Jennifer Monroe, Hayward Jones's high school sweetheart; and Alice Smith, Jerome Smith's grandmother. She couldn't really be sure who was who. They were all neatly dressed and they took coffee or tea, but nobody touched the food. They were probably too nervous to eat, which was completely understandable. They were being asked to make life-or-death choices in the company of some other women they hardly knew at all, under the watchful eye of a man they knew by reputation only. Regina looked closely at the women as they gathered around the table.

When the last guest had seated herself, Regina stepped forward and smiled, but before she could say anything, the smoked-glass door opened and Blue stepped into the room.

"Good afternoon," he said pleasantly. "I hope I'm not late."

"You're right on time," Regina said, turning to the women with a smile she hoped was reassuring. "Let me introduce my husband, Blue Hamilton."

The women blinked or blushed or simply gawked at him, but nobody said a word.

"Good afternoon," Blue said, bowing slightly. "I thank you for responding to our invitation on such short notice."

"Who you think is gonna tell you no, Mr. Hamilton?" a young woman with a honey blond weave pulled back into a neat ponytail said with a smile that was more nervous than flirtatious.

"Well, Miss Brownlee," Blue said, calling her by her name, as if he had done it a hundred times before. "I hope that means we're going to be able to work together on a problem I'm having with some young men whose names I think you already know."

As he spoke, he walked over to stand beside Regina.

"I don't know what you talkin' about," Kendra said, tossing that ponytail and meeting his eyes defiantly.

"Didn't you sign a contract to be a character witness for Lance Johnson III?"

The other four women looked at Kendra and held on to the handles of their china cups for dear life.

"Or not," she said.

Blue frowned slightly. "Or not what?"

"Or not to be a witness for him."

"She was very clear about that," one of the younger women said, and another one, also one of the younger ones, nodded. "She said we weren't required one way or the other. It was totally up to us."

"I see," Blue said. "Are you Jennifer Monroe?"

The first girl blushed and nodded. "Yes."

"What else did she say?"

"She told us that the guys had signed up for a really important, top secret assignment," Jennifer said, and the others nodded in agreement. "And as part of their file, they had to list a woman who would testify to their good character, if the need ever arose and if we . . . How did she put it?"

"If we were so moved," the other girl responded. "I remember because it sounded kind of formal. When I asked her what that meant exactly, she said all we had to do was give our honest opinion of the guys if anybody ever asked us and be prepared to swear to it. I said okay, and then she gave me fifty thousand cash and told me when he graduated, there was two hundred thousand more where that came from."

The others nodded again, and some actually sighed at the mention of the money, almost like some women will coo at an infant, moved in some primal way that they can't control.

"What was the money for?" Regina asked.

"I'm not sure exactly," Judy said slowly. "They said it was kind of like insurance money since the top secret job the guys had to do was dangerous and they thought it was only fair."

"Did that make sense to you?"

She shrugged. "He's the one who put my name down, so I figured he knew what he was doing."

"Did you tell him about Ms. Mayflower coming to see you?"

"No."

"Why not?"

"She asked us not to mention it," said the oldest of the women.

"Mrs. Smith?" Blue said.

Jerome Smith's grandmother nodded.

"And you just went along without wondering why?"

"I don't know about you, Mr. Hamilton," said the last woman to speak, which would make her Louise Solomon, Jackson Stevens's neighbor. "But where I'm from, fifty thousand falling in your lap out of the sky clears up more questions than it raises."

"And it wasn't like I was still seeing him anymore," Jennifer added. "By the time that woman came by, he had left me for a girl he started sneaking around with freshman week, even though I gave up a scholarship to Yale Drama School to follow him down here!"

Even four years later, she was clearly still angry.

"Why did you do it?" Regina said.

"Do what?"

"Give up your scholarship."

Jennifer looked at Regina and her eyes filled up with tears. "I loved him," she said softly. "He was my first."

"See, that's what happens," Kendra said. "You fall in love wit 'em and all they do is take advantage of you."

Regina knew that it was not a good sign that nobody disagreed. "What do you mean?"

"Look, I loved Lance," Kendra said, sounding weary of the whole topic, "and I thought he loved me, too. When I got pregnant all of a sudden, he acted like I was the biggest slut in Atlanta." She tossed her hair for emphasis. "All those Morehouse guys are like that. They don't respect girls from Atlanta, even when they chasin' after us."

"They don't respect girls, *period*," said Jennifer. "It doesn't even matter where you're from."

"All I know is that he told everybody I had been with all his boys, so how did he know it was his baby anyway?"

The other women were watching her intently. Mrs. Solomon clucked her tongue sympathetically.

"I was dancin' at the clubs just to make ends meet and you can't do that once you start showing, so I moved back in with my mama. Once the baby came, he act like he didn't even have no son. He never paid one dime and never even laid eyes on my baby's face. When that woman told me he had put my name down as the beneficiary for all that money, I figured it was his way of finally taking responsibility. That money will give my baby a real future. I'm not throwing that away because all of a sudden his daddy is tryin' to back out of the deal he made. That's his problem, not mine."

"What did they tell you about the project the boys signed on to be a part of?" Blue said. "Did they give you any details at all?"

"She said something about a space station," Louise Solomon said. "That they might be gone for a long time."

"Now they don't want to go," Judy Hughes said. "But you know what? Nobody twisted their arms, Mr. Hamilton, just like nobody twisted ours."

She fiddled with her cup for a minute then put it down. "The truth is, Stan Hodges owes me. He owes me big time."

"And why is that?" Blue said quietly.

"Because he stole my research." She practically spat out the words. "Freshman year, we were lab partners. He was good at chemistry, but not as good as I was, so the professor asked if I would tutor him so he wouldn't lose his scholarship. He said he really appreciated it, and asked me a lot of questions about my work since I was already doing independent research. I was trying to get a grant so I could stay in school and he knew that, so when I shared my research with him, he was always so interested and supportive. And you know what he did? He stole everything and used it to submit an early submission grant to the same foundation I was trying for and he got it! When my proposal came up for review, they not only turned me down, they cautioned me about claiming another student's work as my own."

"Why didn't you show them your original research?" Regina asked. "Wouldn't that have proven you were the rightful owner?"

"There was a fire in the lab where I had been working," Judy said slowly. "Everything was destroyed. There was some talk of arson, but nobody could ever prove anything. I couldn't pay my fees so I had to drop out of school and get a job."

There was silence for a minute, and then Blue had a question. "Do you consider what he did to be a capital offense?"

"I don't know what kind of offense it is," Judy said. "I know I wanted to be a doctor and now I'm working at Macy's. When he put my name down on that contract, we were friends. I never would have considered saying a word against him. But after the way he treated me? I don't care what happens to him."

"I don't think you would say that if you knew all the facts," Blue said. "There's no way to make this any easier, so I'm just going to tell you what I know. This person who came to see all of you with that contract you signed is not a woman. She's a vampire."

Regina had expected them to recoil, maybe even to faint or scream or start calling on God for protection, but they didn't. They just sat there, waiting, as if Blue had said, "She likes to eat at the Waffle House."

"Do you understand what we're saying?" Regina said, wondering if they were in shock. *"She's a vampire!"*

Still no surprise. They nodded slowly, but no one said or did anything. Did they need Blue to spell it out, she wondered? Did they already know about the sex-slavery part of it? Even worse, did they know about the head-biting thing?

"I don't think you understand what's going to happen to these boys," Regina said. "These vampires are looking for smart men to impregnate them. That's why they came to Morehouse."

"They got robbed," Kendra muttered, rolling her eyes at Jennifer.

"And then when they're finished with them, when they've had babies to keep themselves going for a while, they're going to *bite their heads off.*"

She said each word slowly and distinctly. Alice Smith shuddered a little and closed her eyes, but Judy didn't blink.

"I thought vampires drank your blood," she said, looking at Regina.

That's when Regina understood. She drew in her breath so sharply that she heard it herself. "You already know about the head biting and you're still not going to speak up for them?"

In the silence, Mrs. Solomon spoke up quietly. "I have something to add."

They all turned in her direction.

"I'm here because Jackson Stevens put my name down. I'm seventy-six years old, on a fixed income, so I rent out half my duplex to students to help with my expenses. I rented the place to Jackson the second semester of his freshman year. He told me he had just inherited some money and he wanted to pay six months in advance. The place had been empty for a while and, to tell the truth, I was having some problems making ends meet. Everything is up so high these days."

"And did he pay in advance?" Regina interrupted Louise gently before they got sidetracked into the details.

"Yes, he did, and I made some improvements to the place, and then he paid some more in advance and things seemed to be working out fine. I didn't bother him and he didn't bother me, but then one night real late, I heard somebody hollering next door at Jackson's, shouting and carrying on something awful. Well, I am a respectable woman, so I put on my robe and I went outside and rang the bell. I could hear his voice, but there was a woman there, too. She sounded like she was crying. When they heard the bell, it got real quiet. Jackson came to the door. He didn't open it very wide, but over his shoulder, I could see the place was all torn up, broken things lying around like they'd been throwing stuff. And I said, What's going on? And he said she got mad about a text he got from some other girl and went crazy jealous and jumped on him. Where is she? I said, and he said she was fine, just too embarrassed to come out because she's not dressed. So I told him to take care of his business with a little more decorum, and I went back to my side of the house and went back to bed."

"Go on," Regina said.

"Well, he paid another six months in advance just when my taxes were coming due and I really needed that money, so I was glad to get it. But then he started hitting them."

"Hitting them?" Blue's voice was hard and cold.

She nodded. "I never actually saw it, but I heard enough, and I saw a couple of them afterward. Big ol' sunglasses on their face, like that's going to cover everything. He used to bounce them off the walls, sounded like to me, but seems like there was always another one to come in whenever he sent one packing. That's the part I never understood." She ran her hands over her hair and patted it nervously. "Finally, I couldn't take it anymore. You know how it is when you know something, you can't just pretend to yourself that you don't know it, even if you want to. So I just asked him to move out. He really raised a ruckus, too, but I couldn't take it anymore, even if I did need the money, especially when he said he wanted me to pay back everything he'd paid in advance. That money been gone, Mrs. Hamilton. You know how it is with everything so high."

"I understand. Go on."

"Well, a couple weeks later, Ms. Mayflower came by to tell me Jackson had listed me as some sort of beneficiary and handed me fifty thousand just for signing something." She looked around at the others who were nodding at her. "So I figured he was sorry for how he'd been acting, and I signed."

Regina looked at Jerome Smith's grandmother, who was the only one among them who hadn't spoken yet. "What about you, Mrs. Smith? Are you really prepared to let them take Jerome?"

"This is the hardest thing I ever had to do," Mrs. Smith said softly, as every head turned in her direction. "But I am alone in this world. I gave that boy the best years of my life, taking in laundry and catching the bus out to Buckhead to clean up after these white folks whenever I could get the work. I had already raised six of my own, but I didn't mind doing it. I knew Jerome was a bright child and he deserved a chance, so I got another job cleaning up one of those office towers downtown, and I sent him to the same private school where the smart white kids went and he made the honor roll and the dean's list and every other list they got. And when I'd come home bone tired, he'd rub my feet and tell me how much he appreciated everything I was doing and how he was going to take care of everything as soon as he graduated and got a job and then I'd never have to work again. I was really glad to hear it because my heart wasn't so strong anymore and my doctor told me I needed to stop working, but how could I? After high school, Jerome needed money for college. He only got a partial scholarship to Morehouse—he wouldn't even consider Georgia State!—but no matter how much I worked, we just couldn't save enough."

"Was he working, too?" Blue said.

Kendra snorted and tossed her ponytail. "Not likely."

"I didn't want him to," Mrs. Smith said quickly. "He needed to study."

Kendra rolled her eyes.

"Go on," Regina said.

"But then once he got to Morehouse, he got a scholarship—he wouldn't tell me from who—and he changed."

Her voice cracked a little and Louise Solomon reached over to pat her hand. "Take your time, honey."

"He stopped coming home to see me, and when he did, he didn't have a good word to say. Finally, he said he was too busy to keep coming just to sit around with me and said he'd send some money when he could."

"Did he?" Regina said.

"He sent me forty-two dollars. That was it. I didn't know what I was going to do. That's when that tall woman came to see me. When she told me about the money, I almost cried. I figured it was his way of making it up for how he'd treated me, and even if it wasn't, no way I was in a position to look a gift horse in the mouth." Her voice was almost a whisper. "I'm an old woman, Mr. Hamilton. I didn't abandon that boy. He abandoned me."

The accusation hung in the air and Regina tried to come up with something that could refute it, but she couldn't.

"I know it sounds awful, Mrs. Hamilton, but look at it from our point of view," Louise said. "Each of us in our own way opened up to these boys. By blood or by love or whatever, we bound ourselves to them and tried to do right by them. But what did we get in return? Respect? Kindness? Protection?"

"Love?" Kendra said. "Did a sister ever get a little *love*?"

"We got none of those things," Alice Smith said.

"What we got was lies," Jennifer said. "And betrayals."

"And bullshit," Kendra added. "Don't forget the bullshit."

"But now," Judy said, "you are asking us to turn down a quarter of a million dollars because these guys might have to finally take some personal responsibility for how they're living?"

Regina looked at each of them in turn. "I'm asking you," she said quietly, "to take a stand on the side of some flawed human beings whose bad choices should not be punishable by death."

"Well, that's the thing about bad choices," Kendra said. "You can't undo them just because they come around to bite you in the ass."

Judy stood up then and so did Jennifer. Louise offered an arm to Alice Smith, who accepted it, and they stood up, too. Regina and Blue stood to face them. Regina had been preparing to hear about outrageous sins, apocalyptic transgressions, epic lapses of honor, but what she was hearing was so ordinary. These crimes were nothing unique or spectacular. Just the slow wearing away of affection and respect and trust and love. And once those were gone, they were gone. There was nothing more to say.

Chapter Thirty-one

A Bad Precedent

"I can't believe they hate those boys that much," Regina said when the last woman had climbed into the stretch limo without a backward glance so Sam could drive them home.

"They don't hate them." Blue pulled out a chair for her at the table where he usually sat alone. "They're just tired of them."

"That's even worse!"

He poured them each a cup of espresso and sat down across from her.

"Why didn't you talk to them harder?" she said. "Why didn't you paint them a picture of how those boys are going to die, headless and alone, on some uncharted, vampire-infested island?"

Blue dropped a cube of sugar into her cup. He took his black.

"Because it wouldn't have done a bit of good. If they still had enough feeling to hate them, I might have had something to work with, but when a woman is really and truly tired of a man, there's nothing else to be said."

Regina stirred her coffee and looked across the table at Blue. She knew he was right. He had learned that from her.

"So what are we going to do?"

He swallowed the espresso in one steaming gulp and set the cup down gently.

"Serena and her girls are coming to the benefit on Saturday night to pick up those guys," he said. "I'll let them come, and then we'll take care of it."

"During the benefit?"

"They won't be staying until the end," he said. "I'll arrange to have a helicopter pick them up on the golf course at ten thirty. They'll think it's taking them to Hartsfield-Jackson so they can make their connection."

The benefit was always held on the grounds of the old Lincoln Country Club. The helicopter pad at the far end of the golf course was there to accommodate Blue and his guests who required a little more privacy.

"Where is it really taking them?" Regina asked.

Blue slid his cup aside and reached across the table for her hands. "We don't have to talk about this anymore."

"I don't want to talk about it any more than you do," she said, "but anything I make up on my own is probably going to be even scarier than whatever you've got in mind, so why don't you go ahead and tell me. I can take it."

He looked at her and she could see him considering the options. Their deal was that any question she had nerve enough to ask, he had nerve enough to answer. And she was asking this one.

"All right," he said. "There's only one way to kill them and it hasn't changed as long as they've been around. You have to drive a wooden stake through their hearts and bury them nine feet deep."

Regina put her hands over her ears without knowing she was going to. She had asked the question and he had definitely answered it. She just needed a minute of silence to absorb the words. To think about how that whole scene would play out. What would it look like? Would they run? Would they fight back? Would they bite?

Blue was watching her silently. His eyes were the clearest turquoise, as if his soul was at peace with what he was now required to do. She pulled her hands away slowly and drew in a deep breath.

"They're not human, Gina," he said. "I can't let them take these guys, as sorry as they are. It sets a bad precedent."

"I know," she said, "but they *look* like women. Really tall, weird-looking women, but still the idea of you driving a stake through a woman's heart . . ."

"They're vampires, baby," he said gently. "They've got to go."

How could she tell him how much the pictures flashing through her mind frightened her? A fight to the death between the man she loved and a bunch of vampires? She found herself wondering more and more about the specifics. How big a stake? What kind of wood? She closed her eyes again.

"I'm going to call Ms. Mayflower to tell her she was right about the witnesses," Blue said. "And tell her she can collect her boys at the benefit just as she had requested. That will be her last chance to call the whole thing off."

Neither one of them considered that a real possibility.

"Isn't there any other way?"

"I don't think so," Blue said. "But if you come up with anything, let me know."

Chapter Thirty-two

A Good-Man Story

Wednesday

Before he met Blue and Henry at the West End News, Peachy went by Club Zebra to check on preparations for the benefit and found Iona Williams, this year's chairperson, overseeing the delivery and proper arranging of additional tables and chairs to handle the overflow crowd. Tickets were already scarce because everybody in West End *had* to be there. Tables went first, then single tickets sales, and then people started begging for standing room at the bar. Then the Too Fine Five announced their intention to grace the proceedings and to drop the largest single donation the benefit committee had ever received. After that, the phones started ringing off the hook, and so many people wanted to come that Zeke Burnett, the club's creator and proprietor, set up a giant video screen in the upstairs ballroom so that anyone who couldn't get a seat in the club, which took up most of the building's ground floor, could still be close enough to mix and mingle.

Miss Iona, as everyone in West End called her, stopped giving directions to her crew long enough to hug Peachy and assure him that she was on top of things. Not that he had doubted it. When his responsibilities at Sweet Abbie's didn't leave him enough time to pull together the benefit, Miss Iona was the only person he called. She had been working with him from the beginning, and for the past few years it was her vision that took things to the next level.

When Peachy told her that Blue was going to add five Morehouse seniors in tuxes to her staff for the night to help with the overflow crowd, she was delighted. "They can be our official greeters," she said, making a note in a tiny spiral pad hanging around her neck on a silver chain. "Nothing makes people feel special like being greeted by a man in a nice tuxedo. Tell Blue I owe him one."

"How about me?" Peachy said in mock reproach. "I'm the one who's going to have to find them some formal clothes at the last minute."

"Stop complaining, Peachy Nolan," she said. "You got enough white dinner jackets in your own closet to outfit half the men in West End without ever darkening the doorsteps at Genghis Formal Rentals."

"They ain't ready for my look yet," Peachy said. "First they gotta master the basics."

The basics were about all they could expect only two days out, Peachy said when he got the request, but Blue said it was important to keep the vamps as tranquil as possible. If they arrived and didn't see the guys right away, they might suspect something was up. This way, with all five boys in plain sight, the vamps would relax and whatever went down would be a lot easier to handle. That made sense to Peachy and he called around to a few places and got things lined up for a fitting that evening and a rush job on the alternations so he could pick everything up on Saturday morning.

Once he got that straightened out, he stopped by the lumberyard and picked up six hardwood stakes, all sharpened to a point at both ends. At just under two feet, the length Blue had requested, they fit perfectly into a bright red souvenir golf bag somebody had given Peachy after a Savannah golf tournament that concluded with a banquet on the island. He had tossed it in the trunk of his car intending to pass it on to one' of his friends who actually played the game. Now he realized, he might have a use for it after all. He dropped the stakes carefully into the bag. He didn't want to think about what they were going to have to do with those sharpened sticks and he sure didn't want Abbie thinking about it. He stashed the bag in the back of a closet at Abbie's house, safely out of sight, until he got further instructions from Blue.

"Why'd you put them in a golf bag?" Henry wanted to know as Peachy gave Blue the update on his to-do list. "You don't even play golf."

"Where do you expect me to put them, man?" Peachy said, sounding a little annoyed. He didn't really think Henry had the right to ask questions yet. He hadn't been around long enough. "It ain't like I can stick it in the case with my guitar."

"Henry will come by and pick up the bag later," Blue said, cutting off their exchange. "You got it from there?"

Henry nodded.

Blue looked at his watch. "The guys will be here in a few minutes. Any questions?"

Henry spoke up again. "Were you able to find out anything about the bleeding?"

Blue shook his head. "Nothing definitive, so be prepared to clean up afterward."

Peachy shook his head. "Damn!"

"What?"

"Nothing. I'd just like to kick those boys' young asses for getting us caught up in this crazy shit."

Blue shrugged. "It was bound to happen sooner or later. Once the vamps showed up in that rap video, it was just a matter of time."

"So you think this is going to happen again?" Peachy said.

"I don't know." Blue looked at his friend, wishing he could give a different answer. "But if they do, we'll be ready."

Henry and Peachy looked at each other and back at Blue.

"Oh, yeah, we'll be ready," Peachy said.

"Good." Blue turned to Henry. "Why don't you go bring these guys around so we can get this over with? I don't want to spend any more time with them than I have to."

Henry closed the door behind him and headed toward the café, where Jake had been told to keep an eye on the boys until they were called.

"You sound like you're as tired of these fools as I am," Peachy said.

"I just have to keep reminding myself that I'm not doing it for them," Blue said. "I'm doing it for us."

Peachy frowned. "How you figure that?"

Blue stood and took his empty espresso cup over to the bar. When he turned back to Peachy he sounded weary. "You know, I stood here yesterday for an hour and listened to five different women tell me about the men in their lives and not one of those women had a good-man story. Not one."

Peachy wasn't as surprised as he wanted to be. "Puts a lot more weight than we need on those of us who've still got some sense, I guess."

"But that means something," Blue said. "It means something I hadn't let myself really think about before."

"What's that?" Peachy didn't like to hear that tone in Blue's voice. Blue was about solutions, not regrets.

"I've been focused on the really bad guys, the ones who are the most dangerous," Blue said. "The ones who are already so damaged that nothing I can say or do can change the way they cut a path through the world. Those are the ones I know how to handle, and if I'm ever called upon to answer for what I've done to get them out of West End, I have nothing to hide."

Peachy turned in his chair and looked at his friend. "Twelve years ago when they let that fiend walk free after he killed my baby sister, and who even knows to this day how many other black women, *you stepped up*. When nobody did a damn thing, you took responsibility, and you made the men around here act like men."

"I guess I should have remembered to spread the word a little more."

Peachy shook his head. "It ain't like these boys ain't been told, Blue. They just didn't choose to listen."

Outside in the hallway, they could hear Henry and the students approaching. Blue stood up and buttoned his jacket, his eyes clearing along with his thoughts. Peachy could see him considering the options and making his decision.

"So what are you going to do with them?" Peachy said.

"There's only one thing to do," Blue said. "I'm going to teach them how to listen."

Chapter Thirty-three

Between Humans and Vamps

Iona Williams knew that if anybody had six silver candelabra lying around the house, it would be Abbie. Anyone who had taken any of Abbie's classes or gone on her retreats knew that candles played a big part in setting the mood that Abbie was so good at creating. Her admirers all over the country often sent her beautiful candles and all manner of lovely holders for them, so she had an eclectic collection that grew with each new group that passed through the ocean room and wanted to say thank you by leaving something beautiful behind.

The idea of collecting things did not appeal to Abbie, no matter how beautiful those things were, but the lovingly chosen, carefully packed gifts from women whose lives she had touched moved her and strengthened her resolve. She would send them handwritten thank-you notes and welcome the new addition. When Iona asked if she could borrow some of Abbie's silver to make sure the overflow ballroom was as beautiful and festive as the club downstairs, she agreed immediately and promised to polish up the showpieces and bring them over later that afternoon.

"That would be great," Iona said. "I want you to take a look at everything anyway and tell me what you think. This is the biggest crowd we've ever had."

"I told Peachy if they keep this up, he'll have to move the whole thing upstairs," Abbie said, wishing she could tell Iona what was really on her mind.

"Good luck with that," Iona said, laughing. "These guys are superstitious. They think it's the Club Zebra magic that makes it work. Every time I bring up the idea of a bigger space, Peachy just rolls his eyes and says, 'If it ain't broke don't fix it.'"

Just the word *superstitious* made a vampire thought pop into Abbie's mind. If Club Zebra did have some kind of magical effect on this benefit, she hoped those powers would be in full force on Saturday night.

"Abbie?" Iona said, sounding concerned.

Her mind had wandered. "Yes, I'm here."

"You okay?"

"I'm sorry, sweetie. I've got a lot on my mind."

"Well, once this is all over, you need to go on back to that island for a while and let your mind roll on," Iona said. "The sisterhood can spare you for a little of that rest and reflection you're always urging on the rest of us."

That made Abbie smile. After she had finally coaxed Iona into trying meditation, her friend had become a real devotee and she never missed a sunrise. It made sense to her that you could train your mind to be at peace the same way you could train your fingers to play Mozart.

"That's exactly what I intend to do," Abbie said, assuming things went smoothly on Saturday night. "Thanks for reminding me."

"Physician, heal thyself," Iona said. "See you later!"

Abbie wasn't sure about her supply of silver polish, but she knew exactly where the silver candelabra were. She always stored them in the back of the closet on the top shelf, lovingly wrapped in soft, white baby blankets to keep down tarnishing while they waited to be rotated out to take their turn in the ocean room. Last year, one of the women who had attended a Tybee retreat had gone to Mexico for a spiritual gathering soon afterward and shipped Abbie two real beauties that held ten candles each and stood almost four feet tall when the tapers were inserted. What better time to break them in?

As she headed down the hall to the back bedroom, Abbie was glad to have a task to occupy her mind. Ever since she and Peachy left Blue and Regina's house, she had been feeling alternating waves of sorrow, fear, and helplessness, none of which were particularly empowering emotions, and certainly ones that could do major damage if you let them hang around too long.

If Abbie had ever doubted it, the dismal outcome of the meeting with the reluctant character witnesses yesterday was proof that the gulf between the sexes was even wider than she thought. Much wider. She was just sorry the consequences of that distance were going to involve some men she loved in an act of community defense that was necessary, but which brought tears to Abbie's eyes. She wondered if this was how women always felt sending men off to do battle against the invaders, and hoped that the things these men were required to do and see and be didn't so damage their humanity that they were lost to their families forever.

Abbie loved the sweet heart of Peachy Nolan and she didn't want to see it damaged by the need to engage in mortal combat with the undead, which was probably an oxymoron anyway. She was glad Regina was going to meet her at Club Zebra later so they could try and figure out what to do to head off a confrontation between humans and vamps from which no good could come. There had to be another way. There had to be something in these female creatures to which she and Regina could appeal, but what could it be?

Abbie flipped on the back bedroom light and opened the closet door. The first thing she saw was the big red golf bag leaning against the closet's back wall like she had put it there herself. Abbie frowned. Nobody had been in the house except her and Peachy and neither one of them had ever played golf. She was as surprised as if she had found a litter of newborn kittens mewling on the closet floor, looking for their mother. She leaned over to peek inside the bag, unsure that something wasn't going to jump or crawl or fly out. With vampires in town, she supposed anything was possible. She didn't see any golf clubs sticking up, so maybe it was empty. But maybe it wasn't, she thought. This was no time to be careless. She leaned over a little farther and saw only what looked like a bunch of poles or sticks of some kind. What was Peachy up to now? Curious, she reached down and pulled out one of the sticks. It was solid and seemed to be made of some kind of highly polished hardwood. Not until she pulled it all the way out of the bag did she notice that it was sharpened at both ends.

Chapter Thirty~four

Singing Backup

"Sit down," Blue said when the boys assembled in front of him as if they were waiting for inspection. They dropped immediately into the five chairs Henry had set up behind them. Blue remained standing.

"I ought to let them take all five of you," he said, and the boys drew in their breath in a collective gasp. "The truth is, I spent a lot of time last night trying to talk myself into doing just that, but I can't. It sets a bad precedent for a man in my position to allow anyone or anything to come into my backyard and take anybody anywhere against their will."

Peachy could almost see the boys slumping in relief as they realized maybe all was not lost.

"Oh, thank you, Mr. Hamilton," Jerome said, sounding all choked up. "Thank you, thank you, thank you."

"Don't thank me, yet," Blue said. "This isn't about defending you.

You don't deserve defending. Your behavior toward the women in your life is unacceptable, and there will be consequences."

The color drained from their faces, and those five different shades of brown turned into one terrified shade of gray.

"Consequences?" Hayward Jones's voice squeaked like he was just entering puberty.

"This is not the time for you to ask questions," Blue said quietly. "This is the time for you to listen to what I say as if your lives depended on it, because they do."

"Yes, sir." They spoke in one voice, their eyes as wide as children's.

"I am prepared to protect you from these vampires at great risk to my own life and the lives of my friends, and in exchange, you will work for me here in West End for one year doing exactly as I say. Do you understand?"

"Yes, sir," they whispered, wishing they had enough nerve to ask him what kind of work they'd be doing, but grateful that whatever it was, it would not involve sex and death.

"Your contact with women will be strictly limited until you have completed a rigorous course of study, reeducation, and reprogramming that will attempt to completely change your inability to form and sustain productive, positive, truthful relationships with women. That will be your primary job."

Peachy admired Blue's resolve, but he wondered how the hell they were supposed to move these guys from where they were to where they needed to be in one short year. He figured Blue would tell him soon enough. Right now, all he had to do was get them fitted for their tuxes.

"Do you understand?"

"Yes, sir."

"At the end of one year, if you do everything I tell you to do, maybe you'll begin to know what a man is and what a man does. And then, if you're very lucky, maybe the next time you need a woman to stand up for you, you won't have to come crawling to me because you can't find one. Do you understand?"

"Yes, sir."

"Good, because let me assure you that if you don't do exactly as I say, you will wish you had taken your chances with the vampires."

"Yes, sir."

"Speak up!"

"Yes, sir!"

"Good, then our business is over for now. I want you to go with Mr. Nolan so he can get you fitted for the benefit."

As they stood up to leave, the panic returned to Lance Young's eyes. "But if we're not going anywhere, why do we have to go to the benefit at all?"

"Because," Blue said, "you're going to be singing backup."

Chapter Thirty-five

All That Vampire Stuff

Abbie was already standing in the back of Club Zebra talking to Miss Iona when Regina arrived. They had agreed to meet there because Miss Iona wanted them to see the decorations and they wanted to see one another. The building was buzzing with final preparations for the benefit, but Miss Iona was the calm center in the eye of the storm. Everything was so well organized that she had time to stop and give them a quick update.

Good thing she doesn't know about the vamps, Regina thought. Miss Iona would have called the National Guard, since her Civil Rights movement experiences didn't include driving sharpened stakes through anybody's heart.

"The press has been calling all day asking if we're going to do a red carpet thing because those girls are coming," she said, rolling her eyes. "I told them the whole idea of a speakeasy is to be hard to find. A red carpet sort of goes against the whole idea of what we're doing."

Zeke Burnett always described it as "a floating speakeasy and cabaret, and the international center of bohemian negritude." Miss Iona was taking him at his word, although Club Zebra hadn't been a speakeasy since the early days and true negritude was as hard to find these days as true love.

"Everything looks great," Abbie said, nodding her approval while Iona beamed. She knew that if Abbie liked it, Peachy would love it.

The small stage was already set up with the bandstand and several microphones. The front tables were so close that the people who sat there would be able to reach out and touch the performers, which is why those seats were reserved for Blue's guests, not his fans. At such close range, fans were guaranteed to act a fool.

"Where are you going to put my candleholders?"

"Upstairs," Iona said. "The art students over at Spelman made a completely amazing Zebra out of papier-mâché that you are going to love, almost as much as I love that husband of yours."

"Join the club." Regina forced herself to smile. "What's he done now to earn your adoration?"

"Well, he knows we've got this huge overflow of folks coming, so he's giving me five Morehouse seniors to help with greeting people and making everybody feel welcome."

Regina knew exactly what five students she was talking about. She nodded her approval.

"That's great," Regina said.

"Peachy's going to have them all in tuxes in time for Saturday night, too," Iona said, as a uniformed deliveryman walked in, all but obscured by a giant bouquet of birds-of-paradise.

"Look at this chile. All in the wrong place, just as big as you please. No, no, no!" Iona said. "That goes upstairs by the . . . Oh, come on, sweetie. Let me show you."

She turned to Abbie and Regina as the deliveryman struggled to turn around without bumping into anything. "Tell Blue to call me if he has any questions or concerns, but everything will be ready for whatever he wants to do."

She was referring to whether Blue wanted to sing or not, a decision he always made at the moment he stood up to thank everybody for coming. Folks always wanted him to sing, but he never promised he would. The anticipation made the experience even more exciting, if he actually stepped forward and nodded his head to cue the band.

"I'll tell him," Regina said, as the door closed behind Iona and she turned to Abbie. "Shall we sit for a minute?"

Abbie pulled out a chair at the closest table. "Absolutely."

Regina took one, too. They looked at each other and Abbie attempted a shaky smile that she couldn't quite pull off. Regina reached for her hand.

"You okay?"

Abbie nodded and took a deep breath. "I'm okay. It's just that . . ."

"What? Tell me."

"I don't know how I can look at either one of them if we let them go through with it."

"How can we stop them?" Regina had been hoping Abbie had a plan.

"I don't know."

"Those women told me I couldn't understand the way they felt because I've got Blue," Regina said. "Do you think that's true? Am I out of touch with how bad things have gotten between men and women?"

"Of course you are," Abbie said. "You're living under ideal conditions with a perfect man."

"Blue's not perfect," Regina said.

Abbie raised her eyebrows. "When is the last time he lied to you?"

"Never."

"Raised his hand to you?"

"Never!"

"Ignored Sweetie?"

"Never."

"Didn't take his responsibilities seriously as a man, as a husband, as a father, as a friend?"

"Never, never, never, and never."

Abbie looked at Regina with a small smile. "Sounds like perfection to me."

"But what does that mean for our future?" Regina said. "If no woman will vouch for a man when a woman's words are all that stand between him and annihilation, how can we go on together?"

They sat in silence, a small island of stillness in the midst of all the last-minute preparations.

"Maybe that's what this is all about," Abbie said finally, and her voice was very quiet.

"What?" Regina had been lost in her own thoughts.

"Maybe these vampires are giving us a chance to ask ourselves that question."

She sounded so miserable, Regina squeezed her hand gently.

"Blue keeps reminding me they're vampires, not women."

"But they used to be women," Abbie said. "Once upon a time, before all the bad choices and the bad men and the unavoidable consequences, they were women in love, just like us."

That was exactly what Regina had been turning over in her mind all night. If they got this way only in self-defense, couldn't they consider changing their ways once the danger disappeared?

"But they're not like us anymore."

Abbie smoothed the striped tablecloth, a Club Zebra trademark. "We don't know that to be one hundred percent true."

Regina looked at Abbie, who was still smoothing the tablecloth like it was the most important thing on her mind. "What do you mean?"

Abbie clasped her hands in her lap and looked at Regina. "I mean we have to find that one tiny little speck of a real woman that I believe is hiding in there right in the middle of all that vampire stuff."

Regina thought of Aretha's comment about Abbie's deep-seated belief in the goodness of all beings, even the undead. "What makes you so sure it's still in there?"

"I'm *not* sure," Abbie said, "but I found a new golf bag full of sharpened sticks in my back room closet and I can't just sit here and let them do what I know they're going to do. I *am* sure of that."

"It's almost like it isn't fair," Regina said slowly. "It was men who made their mother go looking for a spell in the first place and now it's going to be men who . . ." She searched for a word. "*Eliminate* them."

"*Our* men," Abbie said. "The men we love."

And that, she realized, was the real challenge of the vampires. If there was no real possibility of creating anything with any man that could be identified even loosely as a good relationship, what was the point of letting them hang around indefinitely? The vamps' curse wasn't that they used to drink blood, Regina thought suddenly. Their curse was that they didn't believe in love anymore. There was only one thing to do.

She stood up quickly and reached for her purse.

"What's wrong?" Abbie stood up, too.

"Nothing," Regina said. "Come ride with me. We need to talk to Blue."

Chapter Thirty-six

Two Free People

When they arrived at the West End News, Abbie stayed out front with a cappuccino and a copy of *The Sentinel,* while Regina went in the back to talk to Blue. Abbie had endorsed Regina's plan immediately, but they agreed that she should discuss it with Blue alone first. If he didn't agree to it, there was no plan B.

Blue greeted her with a kiss after Henry closed the door and they were alone. "I heard you went by the club," he said, pulling out a chair for her at the table where he had been sitting. "Everything looking good?"

"It looks wonderful," she said. "Iona wanted me to tell you that if you decide to sing, they've got everything hooked up and ready to go."

Blue's face didn't change, but his eyes darkened. "I won't be singing this time."

"Why not?"

"If my mind isn't on it, then my heart won't be in it," he said gently.

"Not even if you're singing to me?"

"I'm always singing to you."

"Listen, Blue," she said, leaning across the table and touching his arm lightly. "I have an idea about another way to do what needs to be done."

"Tell me," he said without a moment's hesitation. She loved him for taking her seriously and not giving her any variation of, *Don't worry your pretty little head about it.*

"Do you remember when I first met you?"

"You mean this time around?"

"Yes." She smiled at his need for clarity, since he had a clear memory of her through at least two prior lifetimes. "When I had just gotten out of rehab."

He nodded. "I remember."

"Well, the thing I didn't realize at first was that somewhere between the bad drugs and the bad boyfriends, I had stopped believing in love. I did not believe that there could be anything in this world between a man and a woman like what I wanted love to feel like." She looked at Blue, trying to find the right words. "And then I heard you sing and it was like a whole different set of possibilities opened up for me. I know this sounds corny, but when you sang to me, it broke something open in my heart, in a good way—not like a sharp stick would do, but like the sweetest sound you ever heard would do. And I realized love was still real and we could still walk this road together, a man and a woman, two free people, and nobody had to bite anybody's head off as part of the deal."

Blue was watching her closely. "Go on, baby."

"That was it," she said softly, suddenly embarrassed to be saying all this out loud. "Your song made me remember the possibility of real love."

"Are you asking me to sing to them?"

"No, darlin'," she said quickly. "I want you to sing to *me*, just like always. But on Saturday night, we'll let them listen, too."

Chapter Thirty~seven

Just Like a Man

Friday

Serena needed something to wear. The benefit was tomorrow and the Too Fine Five had found a little shop in Buckhead that had exactly what they wanted—tiny little skintight dresses and vertigo-inducing high heels. Scylla had been trying to get Serena to go pick out something appropriately fabulous, but as team leader, she had been busy making their departure arrangements and hadn't gotten around to it. Now they were down to the wire.

At any other time, Scylla would have been annoyed, but today she couldn't work up any real indignation. Tomorrow they were headed home, and she was so happy that their endless mission was finally almost over that she was practically fluttering with excitement. She knew all eyes would be on them at the benefit and she wanted their exit to be memorable and mysterious. That way, they would be twice as valuable a commodity whenever they had to return. New clothes were a must.

She had gotten the two of them a stretch limo for the trip uptown and she and Serena sat languidly slouched in the backseat, stretching their long legs out luxuriously.

"I can't believe he hasn't called me," Serena said, hating how much she sounded like a woman waiting for a date. "I know he's talked to all five of the witnesses, so what is he waiting for?"

Scylla crossed her legs in their tight black leather jeans. She was channeling Angelina Jolie today, Serena thought. Always a good look for her.

"He's trying to come up with a suitable plan B," Scylla said. "None of those women gave him the time of day, or he would have been on the phone immediately, I can tell you that. All he's trying to do now is save face. He doesn't want to hear you say I told you so." And she hissed a little at the thought.

"I wish I could believe that's all it is," Serena said, as the car moved slowly through Atlanta's regular midday traffic snarl.

"What else could it be?" Scylla examined her bright red fingernails calmly. "You don't think he's planning to drive stakes through our hearts or anything, do you?"

The thought had occurred to Serena, but she had dismissed it. None of the men they had known in New Orleans had ever tried it, and these kids from Morehouse were just that—kids. They were no match for the vamps and they knew it. As for Blue? It just didn't seem to be his style, Serena decided.

"No, I don't think he's planning anything like that."

"I can practically guarantee it," Scylla said. "His wife is not about to have that image play out in her mind for the rest of their life together. It sort of messes with that romanticized image she has of him as her knight in shining armor."

Serena looked at her friend. "The knight is always allowed to kill the dragons."

Scylla sat up, tossed her hair back, and struck one of the famous Too Fine Five's patented poses. "Do I look like a dragon to you?"

They shared a hiss and Serena felt herself getting into the spirit of the outing when her phone rang. The number was a private line that Blue had given her the day they met.

"Mr. Hamilton," she said, locking eyes with Scylla, "what can I do for you?"

"I've met with the women whose names are listed on your contract," Blue said, "and not one is prepared to bear public witness to the value of these men."

"I'm not surprised," Serena said, "but I sense that you are."

"I'm disappointed," Blue said, "but that is not why I'm calling."

Scylla leaned over so that she could get closer to the phone. Up front on the other side of the glass, the driver eased through the crowded streets as if he was the only car on the road.

"Why are you calling?" Serena said.

"Because I can't let you take those boys against their will," Blue said. "I don't care what they signed."

Serena frowned slightly. "You agreed to our terms, Mr. Hamilton. I hardly expected you to be the kind of man who doesn't honor a contract."

"Your contract is with them, not with me," Blue said. "I'm calling to accept your earlier offer."

Scylla raised her eyebrows and opened her mouth, but Serena held up a slender hand for silence.

"And what offer was that?"

"The one where you take me back with you and leave the young men alone."

Scylla mimed *hooray*, and pumped a bony fist in the air.

"Are you sure about this, Mr. Hamilton?" Serena said, trying to keep her voice calm. "You know you will not be allowed to return here ever."

"I'm sure."

"What about your wife?" Serena said, as Scylla leaned in even closer.

"My wife doesn't get a vote," Blue said, his voice containing a warning rumble.

"I see," Serena said. "We are scheduled to leave by helicopter from your benefit in order to make our connection."

"I'll be ready," Blue said.

"Do I have your word?"

"Yes."

Serena could hardly believe her ears. She was acutely aware of Scylla watching her and hoped her face did not betray how excited she was by this news. "We'll plan to arrive around nine."

"Tell your driver to come to the stage door. I'll meet you there."

"Fine," she said. "We'll see you tomorrow."

Serena dropped her phone back in her bag and looked at Scylla. "You heard that, right?"

Scylla nodded.

Serena still didn't quite believe it. "He's coming back with us, right?"

"Isn't that just like a man?" Scylla said, without answering the question. "He can't just let us take what we want. He's got to make it a contest where he still gets to be the great man of honor, sacrificing everything for his people."

Serena looked at her. "Well, that is what he's doing, isn't it?"

Scylla fluttered her hands in a graceful, agitated motion. "A lot of men would love to spend their lives on an island fucking fine women for a living. And he's not even going to have an expiration date, according to the deal you've made. He can keep living like a king for another forty or fifty years."

Serena was looking out the window as the driver turned into the valet parking at Phipps Plaza, Atlanta's snootiest mall, for no real reason other than the Saks Fifth Avenue that anchors one end and the Lord & Taylor that's down at the other—relics of a time when white ladies wore gloves for lunch at Rich's Magnolia Room, and black ladies were allowed only in the kitchen.

"I can't believe she's going to let him go," she said. "I guess all that talk about love doesn't come down to much after all."

"How's she going to stop him?" Scylla said, running a comb through her already toss-worthy mane, as the driver got out to open her door. People were slowing down, attempting to peer inside while trying to look as if they weren't interested.

"I don't know," Serena said, slipping on her sunglasses. "But no woman gives up a man that good without a fight."

"Well, we gave up five boys in their sexual prime to get him. I hope he's as good a breeder as you think he's going to be. We're putting all our eggs in one basket, no pun intended."

Scylla's words were like a splash of cold water on Serena's daydreams, which she had barely acknowledged to herself, about what it might be like to be intimate with Blue Hamilton once they got him back to the island. The problem was, in those innocent fantasies she was the only vamp that he was servicing. Now she suddenly started thinking about how many times a month she'd be able to have sex with Blue Hamilton without drawing attention to herself. He was going to be their prize breeder and he belonged to every woman who wanted a daughter with turquoise eyes and an ancient soul. She suddenly started wondering if she was jealous of her sisters. *But how could she be?* Vampires don't feel jealousy.

She took a deep breath, knowing she needed to calm down so she could complete this mission with no mistakes. This would be her finest hour. She could figure out the rest later.

"I'm sure he'll be fine," Serena said. *Too fine.* That was the problem. She was already mentally mooning over him like a starstruck schoolgirl.

"Ready?" Scylla swung her leather-clad legs out of the car, and looked back over her shoulder at Serena.

"Ready!"

They stepped out into the spring sunshine like any other thin, seven-foot shoppers out with their driver on a Good Friday afternoon, and so they were, except for the head-biting thing. But nobody's perfect, Serena thought, linking her arm with Scylla as the cellphone cameras went berserk.

"Now let's go find me a killer dress."

Scylla hissed softly. "You took the words right out of my mouth."

Chapter Thirty~eight

Send Me

That night, Blue and Peachy had a rehearsal to which Regina and Abbie were not invited. Regina put Sweetie to bed and made a fire in the fireplace, more for comfort than for warmth, and curled up on the sofa to sort through her thoughts and get ready for tomorrow. She closed her eyes and took a deep, slow breath.

If she was asking Blue to melt a vamp's cold heart with the beauty of his love song, Regina knew that as the designated listener, she had to be open and calm and ready to receive it. She had to affirm the wonder and the weight of it, to embrace the sweet surrender of it. She had to be strong enough to meet the force of his love with the promise of her own.

She was asking Blue to testify in public to the revealing, revolutionary, redemptive power of real love, and in return she would agree to be his amen corner, his living water, his sweet honey in the rock. She opened her eyes, stretched, and smiled. That was Abbie in her head, talking about *living water* and *sweet honey in the rock,* but that's how it felt. All she had to do now was let her husband sing her a love song in public, and try not to lose control and toss her panties at his feet like his fans used to in the old days.

Shouldn't be a problem, she thought, going to the kitchen to make herself a cup of tea. *Unless he sings "At Last," in which case, all bets are off.*

Over on Peeples Street, in the ocean room of her apartment, Abbie lit a dozen candles and sank down gratefully on her meditation cushion, releasing a long, cleansing breath and listening for the faraway chords of Peachy's guitar as he and Blue worked out their cues for tomorrow in the apartment upstairs. Abbie closed her eyes and took another deep breath.

She understood better than Regina what was really at stake. Blue had gone along with the plan and told those vamps that he'd stand in for the Morehouse guys, but Abbie knew that once he said it, Blue would be honor-bound to follow through. That's why he had to sing like he had never sung before. Because he was singing for his life and the life of his family.

It wasn't that Abbie doubted the power of Blue's love for Regina. Abbie lived her life with an appreciation of the power of love that bordered on awe, but the power of the vampires was nothing to sneeze at either, which was why she planned to sit right there until Peachy came downstairs to walk her home and crawl into bed beside her. Because sometimes love just needed a witness, Abbie thought. Somebody to testify. Sometimes love just needed somebody to step forward and say, *Here I am, Spirit. Send me.*

Chapter Thirty-nine

The Best Sight Lines

Saturday

The doors opened for the benefit at seven o'clock. By six thirty, cars were already arriving fast enough to keep the white-jacketed valet parkers busy. Iona and Abbie were moving among the candles, lighting each one themselves as if they didn't trust anyone else with this final, finishing touch. The girls from the Spelman College jazz ensemble, in their elegant black gowns, were warming up on the bandstand that identified them as The Club Zebra House Band for tonight only, while the sound engineer checked the mics one more time and gave the technician in the booth a thumbs-up.

Zeke was giving last-minute instructions to the bartender. Henry was talking to the security people. Peachy gave the tuxedo-clad Morehouse students a final once-over and nodded his approval.

Blue was talking to Peachy near the bandstand. Peachy was

always the master of ceremonies and Blue was always the last one
on the program. That only made sense. Nobody wanted to try to
talk to a crowd after Blue sang. The band would just keep on playing after he left the stage and people could dance or mingle or order
another bottle of champagne, as the spirit moved them. She wondered what would happen after he sang tonight.

Before she could consider the options one more time, Blue turned
toward her in the candlelit room as if she'd called his name.

"Gina?"

"Here, baby," she said, standing up and moving toward him between the tables. She always sat up front when Blue sang. Tonight
would be no exception.

Peachy, wearing his trademark white dinner jacket, let out a low
whistle. "Girl, I do believe you get finer every year."

Regina was wearing a red strapless dress and a bright embroi-
dered shawl she had gotten in Trinidad after Blue's song won best in
Carnival four years ago. People were dancing to it all over the island
twenty-four hours a day. One evening, walking home from another
round of parties, the night was so beautiful, they spread that shawl
out on the beach and just laid back on it and watched the stars.

"Promise me . . ." she had said.

"Yes," he had said. *"I will."*

"How can you promise when I haven't said what I'm asking?"

"It doesn't matter," he had told her. *"The answer is always going to
be yes."*

So far, so good, she thought, smiling to acknowledge Peachy's
compliment and taking Blue's arm. "You better be careful there,
Mr. Nolan. My husband is a very jealous man."

She was trying to keep the teasing tone they always used, hoping
she didn't sound as nervous as she felt.

"You got that right!" Blue leaned over to kiss her cheek lightly and
waved a hand at the table in front. "This table still okay with you? It's
got the best sight lines."

She nodded. "Perfect."

"Good. I've got Aretha sitting with us, too, and Abbie."

"Right next to me," Peachy said, patting her chair like she was already in it.

"Where are you going to put *them*?" Regina said.

Blue pointed to the table next to their own. "Right here. Close enough to see me sweat."

Peachy snorted at the very idea and rolled his eyes at Regina. "Listen, I've known this Negro for thirty years and in all that time I have never seen him drip one drop. Why the hell would he start now?"

Before she could answer, Zeke appeared at Blue's side in a dark blue tux with Henry following close behind him.

"Time to let these folks in," he said with a club owner's reluctance to keep paying customers waiting. "You ready?"

Blue looked at the band director who nodded at the girls and raised his baton for a downbeat. Around the club, the candles were lit, the lights were low, the tables were set with their trademark zebra-striped tablecloths, and the staff was in position to make every patron feel special, living or *undead*.

"Ready," Blue said, and squeezed Regina's hand. "Let's show 'em what we got!"

Chapter Forty

First, Last, and Forever

It was seven thirty. Serena, already dressed and fully made up, sat in front of the mirror, unmoving, staring unblinking into her own dark eyes. Everything was right on schedule. The limo would arrive in an hour to drive them over to the benefit together. This was intentional, of course. Seeing one of them was startling. Seeing all six at once was unforgettable.

Downstairs, the girls were putting the final touches on their brand-new outfits, prior to gathering in Sasha's room at seven forty-five. Scylla and Serena would join them at eight o'clock sharp for a fast review of how things were going to proceed throughout the evening; a quick check of their luggage, which was headed for the airport in its own limo so that they could be sure they hadn't forgotten anything; and finally the revelation that they would be carrying only one passenger, not five.

Scylla had thought that telling the girls about Blue too far in advance might upset their delicate equilibrium. Part of her job was to keep them as tranquil as possible, so Serena had agreed, but now that the time had come to share the news that Mr. Hamilton was their one and only new breeder, she didn't want to make the announcement. She didn't want to hear the excited hissing and low whistling that her words would certainly set off among her sisters. She didn't want to have to think about him lying with them for the purpose of making a generation of very smart, very brown, very blue-eyed baby girls. She picked up a pair of long silver earrings and held them up against her cheek. She had to stop thinking like this. Serena knew that Scylla would pick up the vibe, and then she'd never hear the end of it.

As if on cue, Scylla walked into the bedroom where Serena's suitcases were already standing neatly at the door. Dressed in a strapless black leather mini and a new pair of red-soled Christian Louboutin ankle-strapped stilettos, she had pulled her hair back and twisted it into a tight bun at the nape of her neck. The absence of any jewelry drew attention to the fierce red of her lips and the bottomless darkness of her eyes. She looked stunning.

"You're gorgeous," Serena said, slipping the earrings through the hole in one ear and then the other. They felt cool and smooth against her neck. "Should we head on downstairs?"

"I need to ask you something," Scylla said quietly. "And I want you to tell me the truth."

Serena stood up. "I always tell you the truth."

"Are you feeling something for him?"

There was no point in trying to buy time to concoct an answer by saying For who? They both knew who Scylla was talking about.

"I am keenly aware of his value to us and to the survival of our tribe, if that's what you mean," Serena said calmly. She had done nothing for which to apologize. Scylla herself had applauded when Blue said he was going with them. No one could deny that she had led her mission with courage and integrity. They were bringing home a prize.

"That's not what I'm talking about and you know it," Scylla snapped. "I mean personal feelings of attachment and possible affection."

Serena turned away and walked over to the window, considering her words carefully, unable to meet the unwavering gaze of her closest comrade.

"What if we're wrong?" Serena said quietly.

Scylla narrowed her eyes. "Wrong about what?"

"Wrong to think there is no possibility that love between a man and a woman could ever be good and true and healthy and nurturing to them both."

Scylla rolled her eyes. "Name me one man other than Blue Hamilton who you wouldn't feel was a total waste of your time."

Serena didn't hesitate. "Barack Obama."

A small frown appeared between Scylla's carefully arched brows. "Okay, that's two, and for the record, Michelle isn't going to let go as easy as Regina did. Besides, it doesn't have a thing to do with us."

"Why doesn't it?"

"Because we're vampires!" Scylla practically spit out the words. "Because the wise woman who was our First Blood Mother made that deal so long ago with Madame Laveau to be sure that we would never, ever be vulnerable to men. To be sure that we would never surrender our hearts or our smarts or our reproductive organs again. We would never subject ourselves to misogyny and control and rape and violence and constant interrupting and professional football and war and all the other bullshit men do whenever you let them get the upper hand. That is our tradition and that is our legacy. We are first, last, and forever vampires."

Serena didn't want to argue. Her mission had snagged a breeder beyond their wildest expectations, but she took no pleasure in it. The boys whom Blue was prepared to protect at all costs were not worthy of his concern, and winning a contest of wills with him when he had those boys for his teammates was such an unfair advantage that it almost felt like cheating. She wished she could have won this contest between them fair and square. That was the only way he could ever come to respect her and, in time, accept her for everything she was.

"You're right," she said, turning back to Scylla. "That's exactly what we are. And the sooner Blue Hamilton understands that, the better."

"Exactly!" Scylla rippled her bare shoulders in approval and ran a slender hand over her sleek dark hair. "Now let's go show these hicks how it's done!"

Chapter Forty~one

Good at It

Everything was perfect. It was like stepping back in time to a hip speakeasy at the peak of the Harlem Renaissance. The band was playing a set of Duke Ellington standards like the professionals they were well on their way to becoming. Couples were sitting at round tables around the crowded dance floor, watching as their friends— men in tuxedos and women in all manner of silky after-five dresses, evening suits, and formal gowns—showed off their steps.

People came to this benefit every year to look and feel good, and tonight they seemed to be trying to outdo themselves in both categories. Once word swept through West End that the Too Fine Five were coming, people had talked of little else. Even though no press was allowed on the grounds of the country club, the paparazzi were swarming around at the street entrance, trying to talk themselves into sneaking onto the property, but then remembering all the stories they'd heard about Blue Hamilton and then just as quickly talking themselves out of it.

Not that the vamps discouraged publicity. Yesterday after all the tickets, including standing room at the bar, had been sold, they had gone on the Ryan Cameron radio show and said they were going to be there, and then revealed that they were going to contribute fifty thousand dollars to what Scylla kept calling "the cause."

That made headlines all over the world, and the excitement in the place tonight was palpable. *Their godfather sure knew how to throw a party,* West Enders thought, watching Blue and Regina moving easily through the crowd, greeting their friends and neighbors, sometimes standing together, but more often working different sides of the room. It was from across the room that Regina saw Henry approach Blue and bend to whisper something in his ear. She excused herself from Catherine and Phoebe Sanderson and headed toward her husband.

"Showtime," he said with a smile, reaching for her hand. "You ready?"

She nodded as they walked behind Henry through the building to a private entrance where they would welcome their very special guests. "Ready."

Something in her tone made him turn to her. She tried to smile, but it came off a little tight.

"Don't you worry about a thing, Mrs. Hamilton," he said. "I never would have agreed to do this if I wasn't good at it."

"And are you good at it, Mr. Hamilton?" She was glad she had worn a long dress so he couldn't see her knees shaking.

"Baby," he said, as the vamps emerged from their limo, "I'm the best."

Chapter Forty-two

Old Wives' Tale

The vamps unfolded from both sides of the limo, all long legs and red lips and more impossibly high-heeled shoes. They blinked and batted their eyes as if in reaction to some imaginary paparazzi only they could see, and smoothed their tiny little sparkling dresses down over where a normal person's hips might be. In spite of the cool evening, not one of them wore a coat or wrap, and most of them flaunted their bare, bony shoulders without so much as a goose bump.

Blue moved forward to greet the vamps, who shook his hand, one after the other, fluttering in their birdlike way before allowing Henry to lead them back through the building so they could make their entrance into Club Zebra. Blue walked at the rear of the group beside Scylla, but neither acknowledged the presence of the other. There was no need.

"Ms. Mayflower," Regina said, touching Serena's elbow lightly. "I wonder if I might have a word with you?"

Serena glanced down the hall where Henry was in the lead and Scylla had moved slightly ahead of Blue, her long arms spread wide, making sure she didn't lose any of her high-strung chicks in transit, then back to Regina. Blue had said his wife didn't get a vote in these arrangements, but something in the tone of her request made Serena think that maybe he had forgotten to tell the woman that small detail.

"Of course," Serena said, following Regina into a nearby ladies' lounge and glancing at herself in the floor-to-ceiling mirror that took up one whole wall of the room. She saw Regina staring at her and turned away from her reflection. "You didn't believe that old wives' tale, did you?"

Regina ignored what probably passed for vampire small talk. "I want you to reconsider the arrangement you made with my husband."

Serena gazed down at Regina with no discernible reaction. *People in hell want ice water,* she thought, remembering one of First Blood Mother's favorite responses to whining. "Why should I?"

"Because I'm not prepared to let you swoop in here and take my husband back to fantasy island just because you don't believe in the possibility of love anymore."

The words elicited a long, low hiss from Serena. It sounded so reptilian, Regina half-expected a forked tongue to come flicking out from between Serena's perfectly outlined red lips. She stepped back involuntarily.

"I wasn't raised to believe in fairy tales."

"Only ghost stories?"

Serena raised her eyebrows and frowned very slightly. She had no interest in pursuing this discussion. "I'm not prepared to debate my culture with you, Ms. Hamilton. If you've got something to say, I encourage you to take it up with your husband." And she turned to go, one long arm reaching around Regina for the door.

"Wait!" Regina said quickly. "Please!"

Serena rippled her shoulders and gazed impassively at Regina, who took a deep breath.

"Here's the thing," Regina said. "I thought you vampires prided yourselves on your sense of honor."

"And so we do," Serena said, sounding annoyed. "Something you people always have a hard time trying to understand."

Regina chose her words carefully. She didn't relish the idea of chasing Serena down the hallway trying to get the deal done. "Look, I know all your experiences with men have been bad. I understand that. I know you all haven't got one good-man story between you as far back as you can remember—a lot of my sisters are like that, too—but it doesn't mean good men don't exist. It just means there aren't as many of them as we wish there were."

"That's understating the problem quite a bit, don't you think?" Serena said with a low hiss.

"No, I don't," Regina said. "That's the whole point. There are a lot of others like my husband."

"Well, that's lucky for you," Serena interrupted Regina smoothly. "Since they are so plentiful around here, then you won't mind when we borrow your husband for a while."

Regina wanted to reach up and smack this *thing* across her bright red mouth, but there was too much at stake. She took another deep breath to steady herself.

"I didn't say they were plentiful," she said, "but as long as I see even one who can step up and change and grow, then I can believe in the possibility that they all can somehow find their way back home." Regina paused and looked into Serena's flat black eyes. "Imagine what that might be like."

Serena felt a little thump in her chest. It was almost as if Regina had been reading her thoughts. She wanted men to find their way back home, too, but she didn't even know where home was anymore. She knew it was time for a change, but what kind of change? And at what price?

"What if you didn't have to kidnap them?" Regina continued softly. "What if you didn't have to bite off their heads every couple of years just to be sure they'd never hurt you or abuse your daughters? What if you could laugh and talk with them the same way you do with each other?"

"We tried that, Ms. Hamilton, and all we ever got for our troubles were broken hearts and black eyes."

"The same way I do with Blue . . ."

Their eyes met, and for a second Regina felt she could glimpse some hint of woman-ness in those dark vampire pools.

Serena shook her head as if to clear it. "So what are you saying?"

"I believe there is still hope for men." Regina looked at Serena. "And I think you believe it, too."

Serena said nothing.

"In the contracts you drew up, the men needed one woman to speak up for them," Regina said. "I want you to give my husband that same consideration. It's the only honorable thing to do."

Serena was surprised at the request. "Ms. Hamilton, I wouldn't be very smart to make a deal like that, would I? Of course you're going to speak up for your husband."

"I'm not talking about me. I'm talking about *you*."

"What do you mean?"

"I mean if Blue's song can make you stand witness for the possibility of real love in this world, then you agree to leave all of us in peace and never come back."

"Just the possibility?"

"That's all it takes to change how you see the world, Ms. Mayflower. Just a possibility."

"And if I remain unmoved by your beloved?"

Regina pulled herself up to her full five foot six inches. "Then I will behave as the wife of a hero and honor the commitments he has made. You can take them all."

"Including Mr. Hamilton?"

"Yes."

Serena couldn't ask for a better deal than that. Even though Blue Hamilton was a prize, servicing a whole island full of females was a big job, and her willingness to trade five for one might make First

Blood Mother question her judgment on a mission that had already had its share of challenges. But bringing back the five she'd come for, along with a great big blue-eyed surprise would certainly earn her a place of permanent respect.

"You have a lot of faith in your husband's powers of persuasion," Serena said.

"I have absolute faith in all of my husband's powers," Regina said. "And I know beyond a shadow of a doubt that the love between me and Blue is stronger than any undead thing you've got."

Serena found Regina's tone deeply offensive. She was almost glad to have any opportunity to show this woman who had the real power now.

"I've been told our emotions don't register in a manner that you people can read. How will you know whether or not it worked?"

"I don't think either one of us will have any doubts," Regina said. "Do we have a deal?"

Serena held out her cool, dry hand. "We have a deal."

Chapter Forty~three

The Power of Love

From her seat at their table down front, Abbie watched Regina guide Serena expertly through the crowded club to the vamps' table nearby. The other five were already seated, drinking the champagne their smitten fans kept sending over and posing for pictures whenever anybody got up the nerve to ask them, which wasn't often. Mostly people just sort of hovered around and asked their friends to snap cellphone shots without ever risking actual contact with these strange, rippling goddesses. From a distance was close enough.

Abbie was waiting for a report. "I can't believe Peachy sat us so close to *them*!" Aretha had slipped in beside Abbie and cast an accusatory glance at the vamps, who ignored them completely.

"Blue wanted us to be close to Regina, and Regina wanted the vamps to be close to Blue," Abbie said, offering Aretha her cheek. "You do the math."

Both women had independently chosen different shades of purple, but the effect was so complementary, it looked as if they had planned it in advance. Abbie's dress was almost violet with a high neckline and a long, full skirt with a bright orange sash. Aretha had on a pair of velvet pants in deep purple and a lighter purple silk tunic that draped off one shoulder.

"I'm sorry," she said, giving Abbie a kiss and a quick hug. "I'm just a little nervous."

"Don't be," Abbie said, tossing her head in a way that made her silver earrings dance. "I'm sure Regina has good news."

"I've got some, too," Aretha said. "*Essence* canceled the cover. They said they thought the look was too extreme for their readers after all, and I said I couldn't agree more."

"That's wonderful!"

"I thought so," Aretha said. "And they're going to pay me for the job anyway, since it wasn't my fault."

Abbie grinned. "That's what I was trying to tell you, remember?"

Regina, done with the Too Fine Five, hurried over to kiss Aretha hello and touch Abbie's shoulder lightly as she took her seat.

"Well?" Abbie said. "What did she say?"

"She agreed to everything."

Abbie and Aretha let out a huge sigh of relief that let Regina know how worried they had been.

"Did you tell Blue?"

Regina smiled. "He knows."

Aretha glanced over at the vamps again. They were signing a poster for a wide-eyed young woman who backed away from them at the end of the exchange like she was leaving the presence of royalty. "Is he nervous?"

Regina and Abbie looked surprised at the question.

"Blue doesn't get nervous," Regina said.

Aretha raised her eyebrows with a skeptical smile. "Not even in the face of standing toe-to-toe with the undead?"

"He believes in the power of love," Abbie said calmly.

Aretha tossed her head and adjusted the silver bangles on her arm. "I believe in the power of love as much as he does."

"Then stop worrying," Regina said, waving at Precious Hargrove, who was taking a seat across the room. "Everything is going to be fine."

"Aren't you nervous at all?" Aretha was watching Regina for tell-tale signs.

"Not even a little bit."

"Because you believe in the power of love?"

Regina pulled her shawl a little tighter around her shoulders and thought about those stars on that Trinidadian beach. "Because I believe in Blue."

Chapter Forty-four

A Sucker Bet

"What do you mean *the plans have changed*?" Scylla turned her back on the others as they were talking to a couple who had approached them for an autograph. The woman had asked them about their dresses, and they were happy to plug the young designer as they had been trained to do.

"Mr. Hamilton is going to sing one of his famous love songs," she said calmly, although she didn't feel very calm. "If we are demonstrably moved by his performance, we give up all rights to him and to the boys."

Scylla frowned. "We don't get demonstrably moved. We're vampires."

"Exactly," Serena said, realizing there was nothing to drink on the table but champagne. "Which means at the end of the song, we will easily remain unmoved and she will lose her wager."

"She who?"

"Regina Hamilton," Serena said, as if she had mentioned it earlier. "If I remain unmoved, we take Hamilton and all five of the boys home with us."

Scylla cocked her head like an inquisitive bird. "That's a sucker bet."

"I told her we'd take it."

"That's because you're the sucker," Scylla hissed softly.

Serena frowned slightly but her voice stayed even. "What do you mean?"

"You said if *I* remain unmoved."

"As your leader, it will be my responsibility to represent the group."

Scylla's voice was as hard as her eyes. "I don't think you're up to it."

Serena leaned forward so quickly that no one but the other vamps could actually swear she had moved at all, but she got close enough to Scylla's face to kiss her. Her voice was a low sustained hiss. "I am still in command of this mission and the decision is mine, not yours."

Scylla didn't back up an inch. "I'm not leaving here empty-handed," she hissed back. "If your plan doesn't work, I've got the girls ready to move at my command."

"You have no command."

"I've been rationing their tomato juice for the last couple of days," Scylla said. "They would welcome an opportunity to eliminate a few innocent bystanders in the traditional way and then grab the guys before heads stop rolling and make a run for the helicopter. I'm trained to fly it, so the pilot can also be eliminated."

Serena remembered when Scylla got her pilot's license, after photos appeared in *Vogue* of Angelina Jolie in a beautiful cream-colored suit flying her own two-seater.

"Well, it's always good to have an alternative plan, but we won't need it," Serena said, knowing a leader with a strong lieutenant can never stray into arguing as if they are equals.

"You think you're strong enough to resist the legendary vocal charms of Mr. Hamilton, for whom you have already demonstrated an unseemly fondness?"

Serena didn't blink. "Even if what you think is true, both of our interests are served by my strength in the face of this last-ditch effort, brought to us, I remind you, by his wife, a woman who believes he is as irresistible to everyone as he is to her."

"Go on."

"If I remain unmoved by this song," Serena said, "*and I will,* we get six new breeders to take back to First Blood Mother, and I get a chance to encounter Blue Hamilton on my own terms, on my own island. If that's not what the mortals call a win-win situation, I don't know what is."

Scylla's face reflected a slowly dawning realization that Serena was absolutely right.

Serena tilted her head back and gazed through her lashes at Scylla. "I think instead of threatening me, you would be trying to help me focus my energies on resisting all attempts to break my resolve, so we can get the hell out of here by midnight. *Your* deadline."

"You're right," Scylla said, ducking her head in a subtle show of deference and respect. "I apologize."

"You had a moment of doubt," Serena said briskly, waving a graceful hand at the waiter hovering nearby. "That's nothing to be ashamed of."

"More champagne?" said the waiter immediately at Serena's shoulder.

"We'll have a round of Bloody Marys," she said briskly. "Bring them before the program begins, will you?"

"Yes, ma'am."

Scylla looked at Serena as the waiter hurried away. "You don't waste any time, do you?"

"There isn't any time to waste," she said, wanting one of those Bloody Marys not just to calm down the others, but to calm her own nerves as she saw the smiling club owner moving toward the stage, his famous dreadlocks hanging almost to his knees, ready to get things started. She hoped the waiter would hurry. She had of course convinced Scylla that she was up to the task ahead of her. Now all she had to do was convince herself.

Chapter Forty-five

Just the Possibility

Zeke and Peachy took the stage to a jazzy fanfare that was more Otis Redding than Duke Ellington, as people headed back to their tables for the evening's program.

Regina stole a look at the vamps and met Serena's eyes. They both nodded slightly like boxers waiting for the opening bell.

"Ladies and gentlemen," Zeke said, as the band stopped playing and everybody found a seat. "Friends and neighbors, welcome to our annual Club Zebra Community Benefit and Cabaret."

The crowd applauded enthusiastically and Zeke let them.

"Most of you know we're not big on speeches at Club Zebra," he said, when folks had quieted down, "but since this Negro is the reason we started doing a benefit in the first place, I guess I have to bend the house rules just a little and let him have his say. Brother Peachy Nolan!"

Peachy, who had been standing behind Zeke, stepped forward

and bowed slightly to acknowledge the warm welcome. With his white hair against his smooth brown skin and his trademark white dinner jacket, Peachy looked handsome and dignified with a touch of the hipster visible in his patent leather two-tone shoes. It fell to Peachy to place the gathering in perspective every year, and for a moment, the memory of his sister brought a sadness to his face as he looked around at his friends and neighbors and, as always, was flooded with gratitude for their love and support.

"Nineteen years ago, this benefit was started to honor the memory of my baby sister, Miss Janet Cassandra Nolan, by raising money for worthwhile things that people were doing in the neighborhood. One year, we bought instruments for the band over at the high school. Last year, we paid all the expenses for that great big garden they got over there now, thanks to the West End Growers Association and their interim director, our own Miss Zora Evans."

The mention of the Growers got a round of applause. The gardens were an important part of life in West End, and their recent change in leadership when Flora Lumumba moved to D.C. had served to reenergize their membership in a show of support for Zora, who had agreed to take it on for a year until a permanent replacement could be found.

"Stand up, Zora!"

Zora waved and blew Peachy a kiss. "Don't do that!" he said, feigning disapproval. "My girlfriend is sitting right down front and she don't play that."

Abbie just smiled and blew Peachy a kiss of her own.

"Y'all better quit that," Zeke said, laughing, "or I'll never get this Negro off the stage."

The crowd laughed. Zeke and Peachy always teased their way through the first part of the program and then turned things over to Blue.

"Okay, okay," Peachy said. "All I'm trying to say is we try to do our part, am I right, Senator Hargrove?"

"You're right, Brother Nolan," Precious Hargrove called from the table right behind Abbie and Regina. She never missed the benefit, and three years ago the funds they raised had gone to support her reelection to the state senate.

"And tonight is no exception," Peachy said. "In fact, tonight is an example of what can happen when you try to do right, because tonight we will be presenting our biggest award ever to an organization that is on the front lines of struggle to make things more peaceful for everybody by teaching men how to check themselves. Tonight, our award goes to Men Stopping Violence."

The crowd responded with enthusiastic applause. Regina wondered if they had ever considered that as a slogan: *MSV— Teaching Men How to Check Themselves!* The organization's work was well known throughout West End and even though the neighborhood itself had reported no cases of domestic violence since Blue took charge, everybody knew there was a lot more work to be done.

"So while I get Brother Sulliman and Sister Shelly up here to accept this check, I want to let y'all know that the reason this award is so large this year is for two reasons." He held up a long finger. "One, me and Zeke finally got y'all trained after all this time, and two, because of the lovely ladies sitting right down front. Put the light on them, Brother Dixon!"

The spotlight operator swept the crowd and settled on the vamps' table. Their faces remained uniformly impassive as they stood up en masse and waved at someone or something only they could see. The crowd went wild. Regina was watching Peachy's face, and behind his pleasant smile she could see a wariness and a readiness for whatever might be coming down later.

"These ladies were in town working and when they heard about what we were up to, they decided to be part of it by doubling what we had already raised and bringing our grand total to *one hundred thousand dollars.*"

This brought the crowd to its feet. The band played a lively fanfare as the vamps rippled their long arms in fluttering waves that managed to be both languid and imperial.

"Let's hear it for the Too Fine Five!" Peachy said. "It's an honor to have you ladies in the house."

Watching from her seat, Regina applauded, too, and offered Scylla a smile when she caught her eye, without expecting one in return. Peachy then presented the check to a representative of Men Stopping Violence, who said the gift would allow them to initiate new programs for young men aimed at changing generations of bad behavior. The crowd applauded again as he tucked the check in his pocket and went back to his table in a daze of gratitude and excitement.

"And now," Peachy said after everyone had quieted down, "I want to bring somebody up here who truly needs no introduction."

From where he was standing in the shadows at the edge of the stage, Blue looked at Regina and bowed slightly. She smiled at him in the darkness and blew him a kiss. *Go ahead, baby,* she thought. *Show 'em what we got!*

"You got that right, Peachy," a woman called out. "So go on and bring the man out."

"That's exactly what I'm gonna do if you give me a minute," Peachy said over the laughter of his neighbors. "Ladies and gentleman, the rest of y'all, too, put your hands together and give a real Club Zebra welcome to our friend, our brother, West End's undisputed *HNIC,* Mr. Blue Hamilton!"

It was the moment they had been waiting for and everybody stood up again and applauded and stomped and whistled and generally made their love and appreciation felt in great waves rolling toward Blue from all over the room, including the table where Regina and Abbie and Aretha sat, clapping and cheering just like everybody else.

"Sing to me, baby," Regina whispered as if he could hear her. "Tell me everything." As Blue waved at the crowd and waited for their silence, Peachy sat down near the bandstand and picked up his guitar. The sophisticated young women who were the Club Zebra House Band morphed back into college girls, sharing the ripple of excitement that ran through the crowd like an electric shock. *Blue's going to sing!*

"Good evening," he said, his voice already causing visible pre-swooning behavior in several women.

So far, so good, Regina thought.

"I want to thank everybody for coming out tonight and I know what Zeke said about no speeches, but I got something on my mind and on my heart that I want to share with you tonight before I dedicate a song to my wife, Regina."

"Take your time, Blue!" a woman over Regina's shoulder called. "It's your world!"

They laughed at that and Blue smiled, but he didn't deny it.

"I want to introduce you to five young men tonight who you're going to be seeing a lot of around West End over the next year or so."

As he spoke, the boys mounted the stage with their fresh haircuts and rented tuxedos. Peachy looked at them with a critical eye, but found no flaw. The audience applauded the picture.

"These young men came to me recently with a problem. They were about to graduate from college, but it turns out there were certain gaps in their education when it came to the question of what it means to be a full-grown man."

"Teach, Blue! Teach!"

"Because it takes a village to raise a child, but it takes a man to raise a man-child, and it takes a good man to raise others like him, so that's what we're going to do."

Regina's eyes were locked on Blue. She was hardly breathing.

"Starting right now."

When he said that, the boys turned on a dime and reconfigured themselves behind Blue in the classic doo-wop lineup—right shoulder to the camera, right arm outstretched with open palm.

"Because part of what these youngbloods need to learn is how to listen."

"You got that right!"

"So I'm going to give them a chance to stand close enough so they won't miss anything."

Realizing Blue was about to sing gave the crowd the opening they were looking for, and their applause crashed at Blue's feet like a wave of love and anticipation. Excited patrons screamed and shushed one another in equal measure.

"Sing, Blue!"

"Hush, girl! You see that's what the man is getting ready to do soon as you stop hollering!"

Blue smiled and held up his hand for quiet. "But these guys can't just stand around back there, so I'm going to let them hum a little backup for me."

Laughter and applause.

"And if you see any of them trying to open their mouths and sing, you let me know because this isn't a song for beginners to try their luck."

With that, Peachy played a chord on the guitar and the five boys hummed the note and lowered their arms in perfect sync. Several women actually squealed.

"What you gonna sing, Blue?"

"This is a song that people love all over the world," Blue said, and his voice was as low and intimate as if he were talking to every woman in the room one-on-one. "It comes back every couple of years with somebody else singing lead, and people listen to it like they are hearing it for the first time."

He looked directly at Serena, who looked right back while the other vamps sipped their Bloody Marys. "That's how I want you all to hear it tonight. Like you're hearing it for the very first time."

Sitting behind Blue, Peachy was improvising quietly, the guitar weaving its own spell under Blue's words. The boys were doing minimalist moves behind Blue, but saying nothing. No one would have noticed if they had. For the first time that night, there was no rippling at the vamps' table. Every dark, sleek head was tilted to the light, watching Blue and waiting. Scylla took Serena's hand and held it lightly, as if it might provide an early warning system for any weakness or wavering.

"The thing is," he said, "for a long time, I stopped singing this song." Blue was talking so quietly, everybody in the room leaned toward him slightly, not wanting to miss a word. In the packed ballroom upstairs, people raised their faces to the big screen and hung on every word. "I felt like it wasn't fair."

"Teach, Blue!" said a female voice in the back. "Tell the truth."

"Because I realized that too many brothers were prepared to let me sing this song as if they were right there singing it, too, but that wasn't the truth."

"Take your time, baby!" a woman said, waving a handkerchief as if she was in church showing the pastor some sanctified love. Peachy's guitar was an amen corner all by itself.

"The truth was there were too many brothers prepared to hide behind me to try to fool some woman into thinking we were the same man, but we weren't."

"You got that right!"

People shushed the woman who ignored them.

"Teach, Blue!"

"But things have changed and some of us have changed, too. Not nearly as much as we need to, and not nearly as much as we're going to, but enough to make me think it might be safe to sing this song out loud again."

That's when Regina knew he was going to do "At Last." She had never heard him sing that song in public, only when they were alone. Regina felt the blush on her cheeks, and for a second, but only for a second, she wondered if she really wanted Blue to sing that song—*her song!*—in front of the strange creatures sitting at the next table. But then she realized that was *exactly* what she wanted him to sing. If these vamps were going to *know* love, she had to let him *show* love. This was no time to doubt its power. *Besides, he's singing to you,* she reminded herself. *Just like always.*

Blue nodded at Peachy, who strummed the song's unmistakable opening chords. "Gina, this one's for you, baby."

When the women in the crowd realized he was going to sing the Etta James classic, they screamed with delight. They all remembered the pleasure of that first dance between the new president and his first lady, when Beyoncé sang it live, while the whole world got to watch them love each other all over the dance floor as if no one else was even there. The men who had any sense were equally pleased with his choice, if slightly less verbally demonstrative, because Blue was going home with Regina, and all that other love he was getting ready to stir up had to go home with somebody.

"*At last,*" Blue sang softly, "*my love has come along . . .*"

The room was suddenly so quiet, Blue's voice and Peachy's guitar seemed to be the only sounds in the universe. At the vamps' table, Scylla tightened her grip on Serena's hand without taking her eyes off the stage. Serena squeezed her friend's hand reassuringly, but deep inside, she felt a strange stirring, like the reawakening of an old memory; forgotten, until now.

"Stay strong," Scylla hissed softly.

"Yes," Serena hissed back. "I will."

"*At last, the skies above are blue,*" Blue sang, looking right at Regina.

All around the club, you could see people leaning against one another, holding hands, mouthing the words without making a sound. It was almost as if they wanted him to sing through them and to them at the same time. Regina knew that feeling. Something happened when Blue sang love songs. It was as if all the magic and the power and the past-lives wisdom he usually kept bottled up inside came out and danced around whenever he opened his mouth to sing. When Blue sang, a lyric became a libation; a song became a sacrament.

When Blue sang, his voice didn't just offer the promise of good love; it offered an apology for every broken heart or broken promise the women listening had ever known. His voice carried an understanding that made the words he sang a confession of every transgression, real or imagined. A confession that said penance would be paid, forgiveness earned, and harmony restored.

"Sing, Blue!"

All over the club, and upstairs in the ballroom, women were

standing up slowly to sing and sway. Sometimes they clasped their hands under their chins like they were offering a prayer, and sometimes they reached out to Blue as if he might walk off the stage and into their embrace. Sometimes they just leaned on somebody's shoulder, and most of the time, that lucky somebody would lean right back.

Blue walked to the edge of the stage now and held out his hand to Regina, who stood up before she knew she was going to, reaching out for her husband like any other hopeful fan.

Out of the corner of her eye, she saw one of the younger vamps stand up, swaying like oat grass on a Tybee Island sand dune. Then another, and another and another, until four of them were up, swishing and hissing loudly. Serena felt herself starting to stand up, too, but Scylla grabbed her arm just in time. Even so, the feeling was so strong that she almost threw off Scylla's hand and stood up anyway.

"What is it?" Scylla hissed. "What are you doing?"

"I remember this," Serena hissed back urgently. "I remember how good this feels."

"How good what feels?"

"When we can believe them," Serena said. "When we can trust them to tell us the truth. When they love us!"

"Those days are gone," Scylla snapped.

"No, they're not," Serena said, turning away from Blue suddenly and looking deeply into Scylla's eyes. "I think it's still possible, and I think you think so, too."

Scylla hissed so loudly Abbie turned to look at them, but the other vamps had fixed their gaze on Blue.

At center stage, Blue took Regina's hand while he sank gracefully to one knee, singing like it was just the two of them sitting on their front porch swing.

People craned their necks to see but resisted the impulse to stand on their chairs. Zeke didn't play that.

Blue closed his eyes, raised Regina's fingers to his lips, and kissed them softly, almost reverently. The screaming of delighted women drowned out everything else for a minute and then was hushed into silence. Nobody wanted to miss a note. Then Blue stood up slowly and looked around, his eyes finally coming to rest on Serena. Even Peachy's guitar was silent.

People reached out slowly to touch their partners and the room held its breath. At the vamps' table, Serena looked straight back at Blue, gently removed Scylla's hand from her arm, and stood up, her cheeks wet with tears for what had been lost until Blue made her remember the possibility—*just the possibility*—of love. Regina was right, she thought. For now, that would have to be enough.

Blue turned back to Regina, who was still on her feet, holding her breath along with everybody else. Then he smiled, and so did she.

"At last!"

The song ended, and for a moment the last notes hung in the silence, then everyone in the place leaped to their feet, laughing and hugging and hoping they could hold on to that feeling forever. Women rushed forward as Regina hugged Abbie and Aretha and realized they were all crying. Blue was still onstage, surrounded now by adoring fans. He grinned at Regina and she blew him a kiss and grinned back. Only then did she look over at the vamps' table for the first time.

She had said that she didn't think there would be any doubt about the outcome of the wager, but she still had to know for sure. That's when she saw Serena, still standing at her seat, watching Blue, using a clean white napkin to dab at the corners of her eyes. When she looked up and saw Regina watching, she inclined her head slowly to acknowledge defeat and turned away. Regina knew then it was over. She headed for Blue.

Scylla watched Serena closely, while the other vamps mingled in the crowd at the edge of the stage, fluttering their hands at Blue Hamilton and hissing under their breath softly.

"I'm sorry I failed you," Serena said, sitting down slowly. "I will take full responsibility."

Scylla looked at her for a minute and then rippled a shrug. "Fuck it."

Serena was so relieved that Scylla wasn't going to make a scene and start biting people that she wanted to lean over and kiss her right in the middle of her perfect forehead. Maybe she had been right. Maybe even Scylla had felt something.

"Are you sure?"

Scylla nodded and rippled another shrug. "I never was that crazy about boys anyway."

"You know this means we can't have any more babies, right?"

Scylla stood up slowly. "We can have adventures instead."

Serena stood up, too. "Until we're old?"

Scylla hissed lightly and smoothed her little skirt over her non-existent hips. "We don't get old, remember?"

"You're right," Serena hissed back. "We don't!"

And the thought made her feel so good that right there in the middle of Club Zebra, for the very first time, Serena smiled.

Epilogue

Just Wanna Testify

Regina woke up to the smell of coffee and the sound of music. She sat up slowly and looked around. The clock said eight o'clock. It was already morning and she didn't even remember when Blue had come to bed. She stretched and yawned and then she remembered the wild dreams she'd had last night.

It was all so real, she thought. *Even the vampires and the sex slaves and the high-fashion models in black stiletto heels.*

She could hear Blue singing with the radio downstairs as she slipped on her robe and brushed her teeth quickly. He was in the dream, too, she remembered, while running a comb through her hair; singing his ass off and testifying to the power of love. She was sorry she had missed their late date last night, but Sweetie wasn't due back from Abbie's until noon. There was still a great big window of opportunity for some serious *foolin' around,* if Blue didn't have other plans. She hurried downstairs and found him squeezing fresh orange juice.

"Don't you ever sleep?" she said, kissing his cheek and wrapping her arms around his waist.

"Not if I can help it," he said. "How are you doing this morning?"

"I'm fine," she said.

"You get some rest?"

"Your son needed a nap," she said, grinning. "What can I do?"

He turned to her, laid both hands gently on the swell of her belly. "I've got a couple of ideas," he said, nuzzling her neck. "But how about we start with some breakfast?"

"You've got a deal. I'm starving!"

"I'm not at all surprised," he said, moving back to the oranges. "A good night's sleep is practically guaranteed to improve your appetite."

She laughed. "If you stop signifyin', I might tell you about the amazing dream I had."

"I hope it didn't have any of those vampires in it that you were worrying about."

"Actually it did," she said, "but you sang them away."

"I did?" he said. "Well, what did I sing that was powerful enough to do all that?"

"'At Last.'"

He frowned as he poured the juice into two big frosted glasses.

"What's wrong? Don't you like 'At Last'?"

"That's Etta's song," he said. "She let Beyoncé borrow it for the inauguration, but I don't believe she was too happy about it."

"Well, if you had to stand up to some vampires, what would you sing?"

As if they had called in a request, the oldies deejay cued up the Parliament classic "Just Wanna Testify," with George Clinton singing lead and sounding more like a Temptation than he ever would again.

"Friends, inquisitive friends, ask me what's come over me . . ."

Blue grinned and held out his hand. "This one will do," he said, pulling her close.

Regina laughed and stepped into his arms. "That song is too fast for grinding!"

"Not the way I sing it," he said, putting his lips against her ear.

"I just wanna testify what your love has done for me . . ."

And, of course, he was right. It wasn't too fast at all.

Acknowledgments

Thanks to my family and friends for their love and support, especially Kris and Jim Williams, Karen and A. B. Spellman, Maria Broom, Ray and Marilyn Cox, Lynette Lapeyrolerie, Walt Huntley, Jr., Bruce Talamon, Jimmy Lee Tarver, Doug and Pat Burnett, Johnsie Broadway Burnett, Elijah Huntley, Don Bryan, Kay Leigh Hagan, Donald P. Stone, and Marc and Elaine Lawson. Also thanks to Ron Gwiazda for taking care of business, Melody Guy for her patience and support, and Bill Bagwell because a deal is a deal.

About the Author

PEARL CLEAGE is the author of the novels *Till You Hear from Me, Seen It All and Done the Rest, Baby Brother's Blues, Babylon Sisters, What Looks Like Crazy on an Ordinary Day . . .* , which was an Oprah's Book Club selection, *Some Things I Never Thought I'd Do,* and *I Wish I Had a Red Dress,* as well as three works of nonfiction: *Mad at Miles: A Black Woman's Guide to Truth, Deals with the Devil and Other Reasons to Riot,* and *We Speak Your Names: A Celebration,* in collaboration with Zaron W. Burnett, Jr. She is also an accomplished dramatist whose plays include *Flyin' West, Blues for an Alabama Sky, A Song for Coretta,* and *The Nacirema Society Requests the Honor of Your Presence at a Celebration of Their First One Hundred Years.* Cleage lives in Atlanta with her husband, writer Zaron W. Burnett, Jr.

About the Type

Minister was designed by Carl Albert Fahrenwaldt (1864–1941) for the Schriftguss foundry in 1929. Minister is a modern design based on the Aldine types of Claude Garamond and Aldus Manutius. The characters have an inclined stress as their designs mimic the hand-held angle of the work of early scribes. Minister has wide, generous capitals with cupped serifs, making it an easy-to-read, straightforward text face.